HITLER'S BARBER
– a Novel –

Anthony Graham

Hitler's Barber

First published in Australia by Anthony Graham 2025

*A catalogue record for this
book is available from the
National Library of Australia*

ISBN: 978-0-646-73091-2 (pbk)

Artwork and photography by Horatio Saitis © Anthony Graham 2025

Typesetting and design by Publicious Book Publishing
Published in collaboration with Publicious Book Publishing
www.publicious.com.au

1

BERLIN 1938

At 7am on Monday the Wagner household was as usual abuzz with clatter and conversation. Anja Wagner, Mutte, as she was affectionately known by the family, was boiling eggs and toasting rye. Her daughter-in-law Sarah was flitting in and out daubing her make-up, checking on Tom, her dilatory son and taking a sip of Mutte's thick brew. Finally, Tom appeared. To the women's feigned surprise, he was suited and clean shaven. Nevertheless, there was the usual chorus of 'you'll be late again', 'your eggs are cold' and the like from Mutte. Her heart wasn't in it and she fussed around Tom as he sat at the old plank pantry table to eat.

The family lived in an apartment in Nollendorfplatz. It was one of two on the ground floor. The kitchen was oddly at the front of the apartment and Tom's bentwood chair faced the bay window. There was a stream of people heading in both directions and a few regulars paused and waved to Tom as they hurried past. It was a bright morning, but the bleak winter sun cast light but not heat. Most of the pedestrians were still in winter coats and tweed or velvet hats.

When breakfast was over, Sarah and her son left for work. She walked the 3km to her flower shop in Unter den Linden. Tom crossed the road to wait for a tram to Ferdie's barber shop in Spandau.

Back in the apartment Mutte settled into an armchair in the back living room that was incongruously called the front room. She lit a Sobranie cheroot and poured herself a tot of brandy. Before leaving the kitchen, she noticed a group of boys walk past. They were dressed in Hitler Youth uniforms – brown shirts, black scarves and shorts, grey socks and shiny black boots. Their hair was coiffed in a buzz cut with a greasy slick top. Many carried white pine sticks that were hoisted like rifles. They looked sinister, as Mutte suspected was their intention. They seemed to be multiplying and made Mutte uncomfortable – the brandy helped to ease her disquiet.

Tom did not have long to wait for a tram. He boarded and as usual all seats were taken. He was left to strap hang in the central vestibule. There were a couple of young men smoking and talking loudly about their frolics on the previous evening. 'Drunk as a horse fly', said the taller boy to his friend. 'How would you know', was the reply, 'you were too busy eye fucking the fat barmaid'. The men gaped at Tom for reaction and approval, but he simply gazed out the window pretending to take in the busy foot traffic. The men looked at one another, contemplating their next move, but the old conductress rolled up to them and told them to 'shut up with your loose talk or I'll put you off the tram'.

The young men muttered to one another, but they moved to the other side of the tramcar. Tom was glad they shifted. The smell of liquor had been pervasive but was now dissipating. Tom wondered why he was unable to engage with other men. He knew there was something wrong with him. When he was a boy, his mother took him to a brain doctor. Mutte went with them. He remembered the rooms were dusty, and the doctor was an old man with a Jewish beard and yellow teeth.

'He never smiles; he hardly ever speaks. He says odd things. People think he is strange'. Tom remembered Mutte and his mother talking to the doctor as if he was not there. 'And what did the old man say, what was it?

Oh yes Tom recalled that day. The doctor's voice was husky and hard to understand. He said he was a student of someone called Jung and 'your lad has a shut-in personality' and yes, he also told the women the Russians called it autism. 'Whatever that is', Tom now muttered to himself as he had done a thousand times before.

The two young louts must have heard him as they ceased their endless babble about their previous evening's high jinks and turned to face him. The tram stopped. They arrived at Spandau. Tom climbed down the steps and made his way to Ferdie the Barber's shop. He took a quick glance over his shoulder, but the two men did not follow him.

He entered the still shuttered salon and set up his chair. He unpacked his gleaming scissors, clippers and trimmers that he sterilised every evening in hot water and alcohol. He laid out his combs and brushes and checked there were full bottles of cologne, balm and pre-shave lotion. He went to the staff room and selected a newly laundered black apron. He inspected his appointment book and noticed there was an entry at 9am that read 'besonders'. Tom walked back to the front of the shop. Ferdie Verento, the owner, was sitting at his desk by the front door laying out his appointment and ledger books.

'What does this mean Mr Verento'? Tom asked.

'We have visitors, Tom. Very important visitors – Mussolini is in Berlin to see the Fuehrer, and the propaganda department want to show him an Italian business. It is to illustrate that Berlin is welcoming to visitors. They will be accompanied by journalists and photographers. You are my best cutter. Il Duce or the Fuehrer may ask for a haircut. You will oblige. I suggest you leave their ears intact'.

He heartily laughed at his jest, but Tom was unamused. 'Why', he thought would Ferdie think he would 'cut off a customer's ears.'

Ferdie was, by birth Sicilian. He was a minor mafiosi in Palermo but fell foul of his familia when he botched a contract and killed a priest, wrongly believing him to be a carabinieri in disguise. He made his way across Europe and finished up in Berlin with a new name, a twirling black moustache and a forged hairdressing diploma. His striking swarthy appearance and loud unctuous manner appealed to the Berlin glitterati and when he opened his shop, he was an instant success. Ferdi the Barber was recognised as the premiere tonsorial establishment in all Berlin.

Tom Wagner, as a boy, knew nothing of barber shops. It was the old Jewish mind doctor who came up with the idea.

'It could be an ideal job for the boy. It requires a degree of careful skill and attention to detail that will suit the lad. The artistic elements of the trade may be tricky, but I understand barbers work from styling books.'

The doctor had a patient of noble birth who between periods of madness was a habitue of Berlin society. He introduced Tom to Ferdie, who always seeking a fillip to his reputation employed Tom as an apprentice.

'He is the son of a war hero', he told his customers. 'The lad comes from very good stock'.

Tom took to the job. He learned the craft quickly and became skilled in layering and adroit in cutting. He was in great demand by the swells of Berlin society. His strange manner, his lack of engagement and silence was regarded as part of the mystique of an artist.

Ferdie was also pleased. He saw Tom Wagner as a child of the establishment. 'If a war hero's son worked for Ferdie – then his glitter would rub off on Ferdie'. At least, that is what Ferdie thought or persuaded himself to think. As Hitler assumed more power Ferdie watched with apprehension as the Nazis rounded up gypsies, jews and Romanies. Swarthy Sicilians, particularly swarthy Sicilians with fake histories were likely one day to be included in the racial cleansing. Nazi barbers would be easy to train. Buzz cuts and greasy slick-back trims could be taught to be cut by Gibraltar apes.

Tom was not particularly nervous about the visitors. His disability left him quite emotionless about possible harm. He was aware of physical danger. He looked both ways before crossing a street, but the prospect of cutting the hair of a dignitary was of no concern.

While Tom was readying himself for the day ahead, his mother Sarah was busy in her shop near Embassy Row arranging Dalmatian roses into crystal vases for the window display. Her coffee and flower emporium sat in a row of deserted shops and closed costumiers. They were all owned by Jews, but vandalism and fear shut them down. Sarah finished her window display. She stood back to admire the arrangement. There were seven embassies and five consulates within a short walk. The shop was called Blutenblatt, the German name for flower petals. She imported tulips from Holland and lilies from Switzerland as well as Dalmatian roses. She served strong Turkish coffee and a small selection of tortes and confections supplied by local ladies working from home kitchens. The embassies were a captive audience. Diplomats exercised their craft buoyed by gifts of chocolates, cigars and flowers. The hallways of many embassies were decorated by Blutenblatt arrangements. The British favoured roses, the Dutch, obviously, tulips and the French carnations. Sarah was proud of her little business and enjoyed her occasional visit to embassies to arrange bouquets and bask in the praise of housekeepers.

All was not chocolates and roses. Hitler was flexing his muscles. There were rumours of prison camps, obscene medical experiments and worse. Sarah occasionally felt a well of fear, but like the rest of the city dismissed the threat – it could not be true, not after the Great War. 'It is just another rumour started by those damned communists.'

Back in Nollendorfplatz Mutte went shopping. As she walked down Bauer Strasse, she noticed there were now more closed down businesses. Coffman the smallgoods retailer was now an empty shell. A blood red swastika was angrily scrawled across the window. At least Damme the grocer was open. Mutte did not often buy their smallgoods. The meats were generally rubbery and the cheeses mouldy, but it was a long walk to the next shopping strip, and the smallgoods shop there was owned by a Jew. It was probably shut.

Damme was busier than usual. It welcomed the loss of its opposition. An elderly woman was next to her.

'It is good to see Hitler is clearing out the Juden', she said to Mutti.

'I preferred Coffman's bacon', replied Mutte. She was immediately sorry she said it as the woman gave her a long glare.

'It was a joke', Mutte explained, 'jews do not eat bacon'.

The woman paused, taking in the reply.

'I get it', she finally said, 'very funny and you are right Coffman's bacon was better'.

She then laughed loudly and began repeating the joke.

'Coffman's had to close but their bacon was better'.

Mutte was glad to get back to her front room. She poured herself another tot of brandy.

'Has everybody gone mad', she quietly intoned.

2

ENGLAND 1938

In London, in a nondescript brick upstairs-downstairs in Little Jermyn Street, a narrow cobblestone passageway off the Strand, lay the department at the heart of the city's espionage industry. Behind the black steel door lay a warren of offices. The hum of teletype was a constant as was the buzz of chatter and the sound of leather shoes stomping on the timber floors. Oliver Lancet, Controller of European Operations, examined the phone message he was handed by the bossy chief telephonist.

'It requires urgent attention', she said before turning on her heels in military fashion and leaving wafts of hauteur and cheap perfume in her wake.

Oliver Lancet was surprised by the message. It was the last thing he expected. He summoned his driver and set off for Buckinghamshire.

When he arrived at the Chartwell estate he was directed to the lawns beside the gazebo. Winston Churchill was in his usual spot sitting in the shade in his painter's smock with a brush in one hand and a palette in the other. As Oliver approached the old statesman leant forward and firmly daubed the canvas that rested on an easel and stand. He nodded to Oliver and pointed him to a canvas chair.

'Sit', he said, and as if by magic a manservant appeared. 'A double tot for me and a highball for Mr Lancet', Winston told the man.

He laid down his brush and sat at a wooden picnic table while cutting then lighting a plump Monte Christo.

'That was quick, I did not know the Cage worked so expeditiously'? he said between puffs.

'I thought you had retired Winston'?

'Put it down to curiosity or better still a wish that our gentle fields are not overrun with Huns and, I am still a member of the Commons. I wish to find out if Hitler is re-arming'.

'I hear you are never in the House', Oliver Lancet once served, as an intelligence major, under then Lord of the Admiralty Churchill in the Dardanelles. He was one of the few men on the face of the earth who could speak frankly to Churchill. He also knew that if the old soldier was struck by the 'black dog' of his long-standing depression or if he had a tot or three too many the day before there was a risk of an explosion of epithets. Today Churchill was relatively sanguine.

'Baldwin and his crew are thick as a Liverpool fog and as fearful as a biddy at a banshee's ball. I am concerned that they will lead us into a peace we cannot win.'

'But re-arm', Oliver asked, 'would Hitler really be so crazy'?

'You might be a fine spy Oliver, but you do not have a monopoly on the well-spring of information. The Germans are a great and proud people. They are still smarting after their debacle in the Great War. The populace somehow has been bewitched by Hitler. I do not like being in the sights of that gang of misfits in Berlin'.

'I have always thought Poland was their main goal,' replied Oliver Lancet.

'One of their main goals, yes, but the Nazis now believe they are a super race. Their scientists have sacrificed honest research for the evil theory of eugenics. The Jewish doctors have either emigrated or are in jail. One day I hope the world will understand that scientists are as weak and foul as politicians.'

'Save for you', Oliver replied.

Churchill looked at him, suspecting sarcasm, but Oliver Lancet remained impassive as he took a sip of the overly strong Whisky Highball and lit a Senior Service cigarette.

'I hear you have a source on the inside. I am told a General. If Hitler is re-arming I want to know'.

'I have no sleeper, if that is what you mean. I have sources, particularly among the Press Corp, but their information does not come with a warranty.'

Lancet wondered how Churchill knew of his mole. He had been in place since the rise of the Nazis. Oliver was not willing to sacrifice him before the war had even begun. General Hoeven, recently promoted, one day may be vital.

Churchill thought the reply over. He seemed to accept the lie.

'I am not going to ask you how you do it but find out if Hitler has a new chef and if we are to be the first course of the Nazi glutton. You must have a Johnny on the spot. And I hear there will be resignations on my side of the House. What have you heard.'

'There is rumbling Winston, that is all I know.'

Winston huffed and puffed a little and lit another cigar.

Oliver Lancet was pleased the subject of sleeper spies petered out and after refusing a half-hearted invitation to lunch he motored back to the Cage. The Service had an agent in Berlin. He was snug and comfortable at the Embassy. It was about time he earned his keep.

Later that day in Berlin the British Director of Embassy Requisitions and local Secret Service Operative Bill Masterson examined the de-coded telegraph from the London Cage. He was puzzled by the correspondence. The author Oliver Lancet was well known to him. They were both Oxford grads and Masterson saw him as a like spirit. He re-read the missive:

'The old soldier wants a detailed report as to Herr Hitler's plans for re-armament ASAP'.

Masterson lit his pipe and gave further thought to his response. He realised 'the old soldier' must mean Churchill, but what did he have to do with England's foreign policy. When he last heard Churchill was brooding at Chartwell in Bucks. Stanley Baldwin was the Prime Minister. Masterson wondered what was going on. Would Hitler really be re-arming contrary to the sheaf of treaties and pacts he had signed? God, the fellow was too busy killing gipsies, imprisoning jews and appeasing Catholics to be worried about invading other countries. 'Very peculiar,' thought Masterson, 'now how to respond?'

He finally replied with just one word 'Really?' He coded the message and sent the cable to London.

Oliver read the reply and disgustedly despatched the paper into his wire out box. He rang his secretary.

'Tell Parrott I want to see him.'

'Where is Fox'. Oliver Lancet said to Parrott, as he walked in.

The minion, a red brick swot shop man, lived up to his name. His rosy cheeks glowed, and his crimson bow tie accentuated his rubicundity.

'We have not kept in touch with him since he was released from that Crumlin Road jail cock-up. He is lying doggo', Parrott replied in a deep basso that belied his music hall comic appearance.

'I know that. I saw him out of the Irish prison. I want to know whether he is ripe. I want to sit down and talk to the fellow'.

Parrott was up to the task. 'He lives in Speyside in Scotland. He is distilling Single Malt Whisky. His brothers run the family business. They make McGonagle.'

'Do you have intelligence he is there now. I need to see the blighter as soon as possible'.

'I am not certain; he checks in occasionally at his mailing address. collects mail and so on. His pension is paid into a Midlands Bank, and they forward it to a safe box in Edinburgh. Do you want me to prise open the box'.

Parrott seemed to be serious, and Lancet recoiled slightly.

'Certainly not,' he replied dismissing his rosy cheeked vassal.

On the following morning Lancet set off for Speyside. He took the early train to Edinburgh where he was met by a sullen constable who was delegated by his sergeant to drive him to Speyside. He alighted outside The Wharf Hotel and trudged along the Cove to the old barn-like building advertising The McGonagle Whisky on a rickety sign standing as sentry at the front gates next to a quaint wood sculpture of a drunk hobgoblin in a tartan cap holding a tumbler of malt.

Accompanied by a frisky terrier Lancet made his way down the muddy path. Speyside lived up to its reputation. The air was heavy with brine. As he walked, sleet began scurrying across the yard. He raced to an open doorway accompanied by the happily barking terrier. A man appeared in the door as Lancet approached.

'Be damned, what sin have I committed to deserve this', said Tobias Fox.

After Oliver Lancet warmed himself by the coal burner and drank some strong tea made stronger by the addition of a dram of McGonagle he took in his surroundings. The distillery building was a large rectangle of dark hewn timber. The floor was a thick carpet of straw. In the centre was the vat. It was a huge copper tank. There were two men working away in the corner of the shed stacking bottles and slapping on the distinctive McGonagle label. They ignored Oliver.

He followed Tobias Fox into a small dusty office.

'What do you want Oliver Lancet? I am done with your lot. Whisky is an honest liquor. Keep the vat clean and blend the malted barley and yeast with good Speyside water and it will do you proud. It will not lock you up, dishonour you or, put bluntly, fuck with you. I want no more of it, Oliver'.

'I totally understand Tobias, you were not treated kindly. There is, however, a matter of national importance that I have discussed with Winston'.

Tobias Fox intervened.

'Winston, you have discussed matters with Winston Churchill. I thought that old bastard was sulking at Chartwell'.

Lancet detected an opening.

'Winston has never been more energised. I cannot say too much but he is concerned that if we do not make England ready, we may finish up speaking German, eating bratwurst sausage and drinking Saxony Rye. He believes Hitler is making ready to invade surrounding countries. He wants to dominate Europe, if not the world'.

'I understand the man is crazy as a scouse, but surely the German people would not want another war. We sell whisky in Berlin. I have been there a couple of times in the last year. It is a tad racy for me, but the partners do not care if our drams are being consumed by mollies'.

'Winston is not worried about the German morals, it is the build up of troops, the deployment of forces and the manufacture of weapons and tanks that are his concern'.

'That is fair enough, I can understand that', said Tobias, 'but what has it got to do with me'?

'We want to find out what Hitler is doing. You speak German like a native, you have a legitimate reason for travelling to Berlin. Winston wants some evidence to take to the soft cocks in parliament. Even some tittle-tattle would help'.

'I am sure you have an agent in Berlin. I am just a whisky salesman. There are spies in every bar and cafe. There are American journalists who have never written a word. Christ, there is even an Australian spook who is so obvious he may as well be wearing a sign, 'I am a spy' on his lapel'.

'That is the trouble, many heads and few brains. You are needed Tobias. If not for England at least for Speyside'.

'Churchill is a politician these days why doesn't he just lie'?

'Shall I tell him that', Lancet replied.

Tobias poured a couple of drams into whisky glasses and passed one across the desk to Lancet.

'I take your point. I am not worried about carrying out dangerous work. Christ you, of all people, should know that, but my contacts in Berlin these days are whisky wholesalers and bar owners. What do you want me to do, go to Daimler and ask them if they are making tanks or take my binoculars to an airfield to see if there are fighter bombers flying around. All that would happen is that I would get shot, my brothers would need a new Master Distiller and Winston would learn nothing'.

'You sell yourself short Tobias, your skills are unique. You should know that. My guess is you will find the right hole in the wall bar and meet a mark'.

And that is what happened

3
IRELAND 1922

After Oliver Lancet made his departure Tobias had a serious session. The blenders and stirrers were surprised to hear him singing 'Black and Tan Bastards' in a loud voice.

'His brothers said he was a blooter, but he has never showed the signs', said a stirrer

'It must have been the wee sassenach', said the blender.

'You are surely right the man looked like a numpty'.

But Oliver was not just drunk, for drunk sake, he was reliving the shooting, the years in Crumlin Road jail and his odd release.

'Still and all', he oft repeated to himself, 'I was lucky to escape with my life'. British spies were not highly regarded in Belfast during the Irish Troubles.

Tobias Fox joined the Secret Service by accident. He found himself enjoying a malt one afternoon in a pub in Portrush after a hard day trying to engage and teach a class of ginger micks at a church primary school.

The Fox family was a mixture of Romany guile, German thoughtfulness and Scottish bluff. The father was a confidence man. Every year he dreamt up a new plan to make the family fortune.

The coffee beans from Trinidad-Tobago that never materialised, the lost Picasso he painted on a masonry sheet and hawked to a stupid Hampstead dealer and the silver mine in Singapore that just needed a small injection of cash were some of his ventures. The family travelled constantly to avoid confrontation and recriminations.

It was Scotland where everything changed. Tobias was never sure how they came to own the distillery. One story was his father won it at poker. This seemed unlikely. A second tale was that the owner was his father's brother. This was even more fanciful. The truth was more prosaic. Though MacGonagle Distillery was venerable and even famous, it had been losing money for one hundred years. His father bought the business for the debts. To his surprise, he found he had the knack and the distillery rose from the ashes. The debts were paid off. His young brothers were enthusiastic about laying roots and Tobias found he also had the gift of the blend. The casualties were the father and mother who drank themselves to death on the whisky they produced.

Tobias once counted that, before becoming a distiller, he had been to twenty-three schools. He found it worked in his favour. He had a quick and restless mind and an aptitude for languages. He learned a lot about people, their weaknesses, foibles and cravings. His whisky blending was interrupted by being conscripted to fight the Germans.

His Great War had been tricky. He spent a year lying in mud in the Somme shooting Huns, before he was press-ganged by the spooks into killing quislings.

He had proved to be an adept bomb maker. In the last days of the war there was an accident in Hanover. A woman and children were killed. Tobias Fox was given faulty intelligence, but he knew this would not save him. The naysayers and peace spruikers were out in force, tut-tutting, as war criminals were shamed, tried and shot, not necessarily in that order.

Tobias easily crafted a legend. He stole a degree certificate from a dead soldier. He was adept at art forgery, and he easily substituted his name on the document. He chose to teach in the North of Ireland as it was less likely he would run into a victim of his father or a court martial. He settled into village life in Ballintoy and taught the local sons of the land in the wonders of geography, mathematics and even Irish History. The Civil War barely touched the town, and Fox was welcomed despite his English roots.

'They say he drinks like an Irishman', said the old priest to the Monsignor during one of his periodic visits.

'He certainly looks like one with his rusty mop of hair', the Monsignor. Replied.

The priests were greatly impressed by Fox. It was not often they could attract an English university man. When they gathered each evening before the hearth with their Guinness and port wine they chortled with glee at their good luck, tempered with 'I think he had a manky time in the Great War', a mumble oft repeated.

Tobias did his drinking in Portrush. Every day he borrowed the Parish Morris and drove to the Skibbereen Pub. He sat at the bar and drank his whisky. He was not averse to engaging the other drinkers in conversation, but he gave nothing away.

His stories of the priests and paddy youth were enough to satisfy curiosity. Like the priests there was no talk of the war in the pub. The drinkers knew he had a bad experience or two and they were best left unexamined.

Lancet found him in the pub. The civil war was petering out, but the Republicans were still causing occasional havoc in Belfast. The further from the city one went the less the 'troubles' were evident.

Lancet had been working out of Army HQ in Armagh masquerading as a civilian quantity surveyor engaged to cost the rebuild of the factories destroyed or damaged in the war. His brief gave him the authority to wander the countryside at will. All sides wanted their old country back.

He walked into the Skibbereen Hotel and sat at the bar next to Tobias Fox. He wasted no time with formalities or introductions.

'If it isn't Tobias Fox'. Said Oliver Lancet.

'Do I know you'? Tobias replied. He had watched Lancet come in and he recognised a military man – an English military man. He was slightly discomforted by the sight of the man, and he remained alert.

'I know you', Oliver Lancet replied in a whisper, 'and I want you to accompany me to Belfast City where you will kill a man in the name of the Sovereign of England'.

Tobias looked around the bar and though every pair of eyes were on them the other customers could not have heard or understood the words. Nevertheless, he picked up his glass, and followed by Lancet, made his way to the empty back booth in the saloon.

'Who are you and what do you want from me'.

'My name is Oliver Lancet. I am a member of the British Secret Service. You are Tobias Fox, but you are no schoolteacher. Your academic qualifications are expertly forged. You survived the Somme, escaped the noose and bloody but unbowed you have turned up in the Emerald Isle. I hear you are a damn good school master, but even the bog-jumpers and turf-cutters in this Godawful place require their teachers to be qualified. I want you to come with me to Belfast and kill somebody. I need a bombmaker with experience. You come highly recommended'.

'By whom'? countered Tobias.

'If you can kill a Hun with a home-made booby made of rags and kerosene on a bleak Somme mudheap you can surely kill a Paddy with a good hurl from a treetop snug. Let us say almost everybody who remembers you swears by your aim. There was an incident in Hanover, but that was due to faulty intel not a bad throw,'

'Why would I risk my life – again, for your lot'?

'Again! Now that is the key word. The war is over and done with. What was dexterous and brave once is now a war crime. We are in the thrall of the Yanks. Their idea of making peace is to sacrifice a few soldiers on the altar of reparation. When we used your services to kill the plant in Hanover you made the error, I admit the forced error, of not appreciating his wife and children were in the building. The wife was an innocent, the daughter of a revered attorney. Your assassination is now viewed as murder. You will be hung by the Americans, and we will do nothing to stop it. We will deny that you acted at our behest. You will be treated as a rogue soldier, a race baiter and a coward'.

Tobias took in the quiet soliloquy. 'You are a terrible bastard, Sir', he said.

'That I am', said Oliver Lancet, 'thank you for the commendation'.

On the following morning Fox left the school.

'A sudden illness in the family', he told the school secretary, 'I am not sure when I will be back'.

The priests were unsurprised. Teachers came and went. If they were not afflicted by the booze, they carried scars, mental and physical from the war, poverty or neglect.

'You will be taking the boys again Father Caligus', the best educated priest was told.

Tobias took the train to Central Belfast and a bus to the Falls Road. He found a room in a private hotel.

'I am a jobbing carpenter; I have come up from Cork to work with my cousin. There is a lot of re-building to do round here'.

The assassination went to plan but Tobias found the Specials waiting for him at the private hotel. They had ransacked the room and found his plan and the remnants of the rags, the kerosine bottle and the wicks. He was arrested, tried and jailed for life. He heard not a squeak from Lancet. A lawyer was sent to represent him, but he was a pasty fellow who kept squeaking what a great job he had done by saving him from the gallows.

The jail was no trouble. The Somme was much worse. The food was adequate, and the Irish prisoners were generally personable and friendly. Liquor and smokes were on daily ration.

Then one morning the Chief Warder came to his cell.

'There has been a compact made, Fox. We are releasing you today. An Irishman is being released from the Scrubs. We call it reciprocation'.

Whatever it was called Tobias Fox was grateful and with his saved stipend took the ferry to Scotland and then to Speyside. His brothers were pleased to see him, and he resumed his study and mastered the art of mixing the malt, peat and crystal-clear water to make single malt holy water.

A bland letter informed him of his small stipend to be paid into the Midlands Bank.

He supposed he had Lancet to thank, but he never heard from him until now.

4

LONDON

Oliver Lancet remained uneasy about Churchill's reference to his sleeper. He hoped the canny old politician was simply testing the water, probing the direction of the breeze. He sighed; whatever it was he was unlikely to ever find out.

The sleeper was more comatose than catnapping. Lancet had not tried to revive him and all he knew was the man was making a steady, even nimble, advance through the ranks and was now a senior officer. Genera Hoeven was regarded as an expert in Military History and taught at the Berlin Officers College, as well as advising the General Staff from his office in the Chancelry.

Oliver Lancet mustered Hoeven when he was studying at Oxford. A tutor, a part-time spook, let Lancet know the man was ripe for recruitment. The fellow was beguiled by the Cotswolds charm and the easy camaraderie of a village pub on a wintry Sunday afternoon. Lancet was a Fellow of the College and over some bibulous hall dinners he found Hoeven was dismissive of Hitler and his gang. 'A circus troupe of freaks and clowns.'

'You would be well suited to a Chair at the College,' Lancet said over tough mutton stew, covered in a rich cream-laden sauce.

'I am a German. I cannot give up on my homeland.'

'And if Hitler takes power or worse still if the Russian Bolsheviks overrun Germany.'

'That may refine my assumptions,' Hoeven replied.

Oliver Lancet, claiming to be a military attaché, ran into Hoeven again in Brussels at a Military History conference years later. It was not by accident.

Hitler was now dominant. For the moment the communists were quelled though the Russian threat was ever-present.

'Have your assumptions become refined? Asked Oliver, remembering Hoeven's actual phrase.

'Yes,' replied the General, and that was that.

There was nothing since. no contact, no covert message, no secret meeting.

The hatstand on which Lancet hung his bowler was that one word – 'yes'.

Lancet knew Tobias Fox was in Berlin. He heard nothing from him, but this was unsurprising. He told Tobias not to confide in the local agent.

'Masterson is an idiot', was his description of the Berlin representative. 'The man's cover is as a trade representative. Treat him as such. At least he will know the fleshpots. If you must, use him as a blind'.

Oliver Lancet's last visit to Berlin was a year before. Lancet heard there was a panic on. Files were missing from Masterson's office. Was there a mole?

He summonsed his secretary. A booking was made on the mail flight to Lisbon. He was chauffeured back to his embankment flat. He packed a bag and made for Croydon airport. He was the only passenger and sat in the jump seat behind the pilots. On the following morning, after a fitful sleep, at a hotel, he left on the scheduled Luft Hansa flight to Berlin. There were only a handful of passengers on the Dornier and Oliver found himself in the first row. The stewardess had served him before, and she greeted him like a long-lost pal.

'Herr Lancet, what a pleasure to see you',

Oliver remembered her well. She always wore a large bronze crucifix as a necklace. He noticed it was missing. He knew most of the churches were under siege in Germany. Hitler had clamped down. The clergy represented a threat to his power. The Roman Catholics were less of a problem. The Pope seemed to be onside with the Fuehrer. The German Protestants were another matter. Ministers were imprisoned; churches were attacked by Brown Shirts and parishioners often joined the new underground movement. The underlying antisemitism of the Christian orthodoxy sat uncomfortably with their common cause of facing the horrors of the Nazis. The relationship of church and state was an unholy mess.

'I am pleased to see you', Oliver replied to the stewardess, 'I hope you are faring well – in the circumstances.'

She nodded grimly and firmly clutched his shoulder before heading down the aisle.

An Embassy car was waiting for him. Inside was Bill Masterson.

'I thought you were out to pasture, Oliver'.

'Far from it', Lancet replied, taking a moment to study his companion. He never liked the man. He struck Oliver Lancet as a typical Hooray Henry. Greater Public School, probably Eton, followed by an undistinguished third at Magdalen College Oxford. A parent or uncle would have handed him onto the Service and because of a Saville Row wardrobe, a rakish sports car and a plummy Oxbridge accent he would have been enveloped with open arms. By not making any catastrophic mistakes he steadily climbed the ranks until he was granted the Berlin job. Oliver thought, by the look of him, he was enjoying his Berlin sojourn too well. The paunch, unlit walnut pipe, tweedy jacket with leather epaulettes and sleeve patches gave the game away.

'You have come for nothing; we found the files. I had taken them home. Sorry about that. I did not expect the great Oliver Lancet to hotfoot it over here. I was going to cable you today'.

Lancet remained impassive.

'Did you ever marry, Masterson', Oliver asked, knowing the answer. The Berlin agent reeked of it. The man was a molly. The Service attracted them. False masculinity, derring-do and a life of deceit was a heady mix. Lancet was himself single, but he saw himself as a monk, an ascetic. Various vicars sounded him out at school for the priesthood, but he preferred chicanery to chastity.

The great British Embassy iron gates were pushed open by a couple of young subaltern guards and the car clattered its way over the cobbles to stop by the front steps. Masterson took Oliver to his office and offered him schnapps. He demurred:

'May I have a coffee', he asked.

'We will have to go to a café', Masterson said, 'our coffee is as bad as the slop at Victoria Station'.

They left the Embassy and walked to a row of shops set back from a line of plane trees in a pleasant square. It was early in the day, and the street was devoid of foot traffic. They entered the Bluttenblatt café and florist that was a well-lit beacon in the row of otherwise darkened windows.

'This shop survives, but the Jewish milliner, haberdasher and tailor have fled. They serviced the Embassies. Otto Lautner tailored a fine three-piece hopsack and his cousin Stephen specialised in fancy pork pie hats. Pity'.

'And the café'? Lancet asked.

'The owner Sarah Wagner is the widow of Klaus Wagner, the brown baron. He was the Huns second best flyer. Even Van Richtofen, the Red Baron, spoke admiringly of him and Van Richtofen was apparently an arrogant sod. He spoke admiringly of few'.

Oliver looked around the café. It seemed the owner was nothing if not eclectic. There were souvenirs, scarves and a trestle laden with vases of fresh flowers.

There were a couple of old men playing chess at a corner table but otherwise the café was empty. A woman was polishing glasses behind the curved and somewhat incongruous marble bar and showcase. She was tall, slim and carried herself with an odd air of authority.

She walked around the bar and came over to the window alcove where the two Englishmen had seated themselves.

'What can I get you gentlemen and hello Mr Masterson', she said in unaccented English.

'You are English', said Oliver, involuntarily.

'Yes, it is not yet a crime', she replied, with a hint of whimsy.

'Sarah worked for the English Consul-General in Stuttgart, before the war', Masterson said, 'and she lost her heart to a German'.

'And he lost his life to an Englishman, so the wheel has fully turned', she replied

She must have noticed that Oliver Lancet was looking quizzical. 'I have a son. He has grown up as a German. I have a mother-in-law too'.

Sarah went off to get the men their coffees

'Tell me about your agents', Oliver asked Masterson.

Masterson did not reply.

'You do have agents'? he asked.

'Agents', Masterson replied uneasily, 'oh yes, I have many contacts. In fact, knowing you were coming I have booked us a table on Saturday night at The Lady Windermere Cabaret. There is an English singer there, a girl called Ronnie Tolar, she is a font of knowledge'.

'That will not be necessary' replied Oliver. 'I will be leaving tomorrow'.

It seemed Masterson had no agents. He had contacts, too many perhaps.

Lancet was brought back to the present by the jangling of the phone. He hoped it was Tobias Fox checking in.

5

BERLIN

Tobias Fox often visited Berlin. He had many contacts in the wholesale liquor trade and was acquainted with some of the city's best restaurateurs. He eschewed expensive hotels and was welcomed at a cozy private hotel not far from the central city. It was in a raffish area, but his bed was comfortable, and the food was hearty. He spent a few days cementing his legend. He sold whisky, tasted some of the foul German copies and visited wholesalers. He made careful and innocent queries about the state of the economy, and he read the local newspapers from cover to cover. There was a double column article about the visit to Berlin by Il Duce, Mussolini, the dictator of Italy, but it made no mention of the man stopping by a local hair salon.

It was Goebbels chief of staff who came up with the idea for the visit.

'We can take Il Duce to Ferdie's Barber Shop. It is conducted by an interesting fellow. I suspect the man is not quite what he seems, but at least he is surely Italian'.

Ferdie's was scrubbed clean to within an inch of its life. The only customers allowed to attend at the time of Il Duce's visit were a retired Admiral, who was a devotee of Chianti, a senior bureaucrat versed in Roman Law and, as a brilliant afterthought, a young Nazi, Heinrich Beck, who would receive a buzz cut.

Heinrich Beck's family lived in a dingy apartment in a laneway in the Munich suburb of Ramsdorf-Perlich. The young kids of RP, as it was called, had enthusiastically embraced Hitler's Nazi Party and they proudly wore their uniforms to school and paraded around the streets shouting, 'der tod Juden' and waving their wooden poles. RP was never habituated by Jewish people, so the call was largely inconsequential, though some of the older, more sensible, residents shook their heads and raised their eyebrows to one another when the black shirts charged by.

Arnpo Beck, the father, was a sot. He was in and out of jail and the police drunk tank for years until he subsided into a life of semi-permanent intoxication. His poor wife Lydie, a dressmaker, worked day and night to feed the brood of six wailing squawking Beck children. Heinrich was the eldest. He embraced the Nazi cause with enthusiasm and when Marten the local subaltern suggested he move to Berlin and join the Berlin Nazi Party. He agreed immediately. He was welcomed by party members, and an opening was found for him at the Post Office as a shop steward. Heinrich saw the position as the first step on the ladder. He extracted union subscriptions and recorded them accurately while he kept a lookout for saboteurs, spies or Jews. Heinrich reported an old postman to his branch secretary for cursing the Reich.

'It's a bloody circus with Buster Keaton as the ringmaster'. Buster Keaton was a Hollywood comic actor and Heinrich correctly realised this comment was an insult to the Fuehrer. The branch secretary was unsympathetic.

'The old fellow has been cursing the government for fifty years. He used to call Kaiser Wilhelm 'a cooked goose with the mince stuffing in his brain and not up his arse'. He is all talk Heinrich but keep up the good work.'

Heinrich was not satisfied by the branch secretary's indifference but there was nothing he could do about it, so he returned to the shop floor and continued to look out for signs of dissent or insubordination. The Branch Secretary recommended Heinrich to the Chancelry. He gave him a ringing endorsement. When Goebbels offered him a job as an intern at the Chancelry the Branch Secretary was pleased. 'Got rid of the bastard,' he told his committee.

Heinrich already had a buzz cut coif, but he enthusiastically agreed to take part in the event at Ferdie's Barber Shop.

The security force arrived at the Shop first. German officers and tri-corn hatted Italians searched the building and when satisfied all was well the journalists were ushered in. They were lined up around the walls. Heinrich arrived with the functionaries. His hair was to be cut by Jurgen, the senior Nazi cut stylist at Ferdie's. The soldiers stood to attention and Mussolini walked in. To the surprise of Ferdie, he was accompanied by Hitler himself. Goebbels took up the rear. He was nervous. The visit was his idea. He studied the salon making sure all was well.

'I have decided that I will have my hair cut by this much revered firm'. The Fuhrer said. 'I expect my usual barber Herr Wollenhaupt of the Kaiser Hof Hotel will not be offended. I would like your finest stylist to demonstrate his skill.'

It was only that morning that Goebbels realised Il Duce was totally bald, and, in the interests of world peace, Hitler was persuaded to have a haircut. Goebbels, former Chief of Staff, was already on a steamer headed for Spain where he would be sent to the Alameda front and serve as a front-line troop in the Spanish Civil War. The man correctly realised it was a death sentence.

Hitler sat in the chair. Tom carefully washed his hair and dried it with a soft towel. He had seen many photos of Hitler and wondered why the Fuhrer had such an exaggerated comb over. When washing the hair, he realised that his hair was thinning and the exaggerated combover hid the dissipation. Tom also realised Hitler frequently dressed in uniform, so the back and sides needed to be clipper cut. He worked carefully oblivious to the flashing of camera lights and the hubbub of radio journalists. He asked Hitler if he would like a touch of pomade.

'He mixes it himself', Ferdie said proudly. He was hovering around nervously, but Tom was both precise and unflustered.

Tom produced a mirror and showed Hitler the rear and side angles.

Hitler's jacket was brushed carefully. He rose from the chair. There was a hush in the crowd.

'You are to be congratulated on training this brilliant young stylist', he said to Ferdie, 'you have taught him too well. He will be the official barber to the General Staff and will take up work at the Chancelry. We will compulsorily acquire the chair and his tools. To compensate Ferdie, he will be recognised as a compatriot of the Nazi Party'.

Goebbels walked up to Ferdie and hung an ornate Iron Cross around his neck. There was considerable applause and clapping and much bowing and scraping from Ferdie.

Heinrich Beck was still in his chair. His refreshed buzz cut was ignored. He watched Tom Wagner carefully. He did not like what he saw.

6

BERLIN

The Wagner ladies fussed over Tom as he prepared for his first day in his new employment. Mutte was, at once, excited and anxious. She had no time for the Nazis and wondered how her beloved grandson would fare.

'Remember Enkel to count to ten before you speak', she said using her pet-name for Tom, 'there will be dolts who are not used to hearing the plain truth. I know it will be hard but if you enter a nest of vipers you need to wear a steel jacket'.

Tom was not sure what she meant, after all he was simply employed as a barber. It was hardly likely he would be drawn into the affairs of state. but Mutti often spoke in parables and as best as he could grasp, she was telling him to be careful what he said. This surprised him. He was always circumspect. He understood his brain worked differently from other people. Some of Ferdie's employees were able to joke with each other in a rat-tat-tat of chatter. He barely understood them and was often digesting things they said minutes after their conversation ended. It did not trouble him. He enjoyed planning his day, writing notes in his diary and working on his tasks. His customers were regulars. They understood his taciturnity was not due to rudeness.

'I will just do my work, Mutte, I will keep my instruments sterilised and the floor clean. I will have my design books on a shelf in case a customer requires a different cut. I am not sure what you mean when you talk of vipers. I expect the Chancelry will be a fine place to work'.

Mutte gave up. She and Sarah Wagner continued to fuss over Tom until he heard the honk of a klaxon.

'My car is here', he said, seemingly unsurprised that he now had a chauffeur.

The shiny black Daimler was receiving a good deal of attention from the passers-by.

'Young Wagner has done well', 'he was not even a brown-shirt', and 'I always thought the lad was touched', were amongst the comments.

The driver was out of the Daimler and standing by the open rear door. He was a young fellow, who looked even younger than his years, as he was yet to grow fuzz. His face was shiny and smooth as an apple and his eyes glittered like topaz. He introduced himself as Tom Wagner approached.

'I am Gerhard Domme, Sir, your driver'.

Tom sat, a trifle awkwardly, in the rear. Gerhard hopped into the front, and they drove away. Pedestrians stopped and stared, and the Wagner ladies watched from the kitchen window.

It was a short drive to the Chancelry. The chauffeur drove to the rear of the building and stopped at the portico to the Southern Annex. The front of the Chancelry was an ornate stone building oozing grandeur, but the new addition built in 1930 was a brutalist rectangle of stone. There were small windows that dotted the building and even at this early hour men and women carrying files or wheeling trolleys appeared and disappeared as they crossed windows.

There was a young woman waiting at the foot of the steps leading to the heavy wooden front door. She trotted over to the car and almost curtsied as Tom alighted.

'I am Maria Schafer, Sir', she said, 'I am your assistant. Call me Poppy'.

This remark puzzled Tom. 'If your name is Maria, why should I call you Poppy'?

She laughed. It was a tinkling sound, as a spoon would strike a crystal glass. 'Oh Sir, I am glad you have a sense of humour. I have always been called Poppy. It was my parents pet name for me'.

'I see, Tom replied, 'I understand. I shall remember to call you Poppy'.

Gerhard the driver watched the exchange with interest. His boss, the chauffeur foreman, told him he wanted a detailed report on the new barber.

Poppy led Tom, at a fast clip, across the mosaic tiled entrance hall to an imposing arched door with a newly painted sign that read – Private Office. She rang the bell, and they were ushered in by a forbidding looking clerk. There was a large foyer crammed with young women busily clattering away at their AEG typewriters. There were closed doors off the hallway. One was marked Wagner-Barber Salon. They entered. There were two rooms. At the front was a small reception area with three straight back chairs in a row. The main area was spacious and empty save for the barber's chair from Ferdis's Barber Shop and a small black table where Tom's implements and style books were laid out.

'You have almost a blank canvas Sir', said Poppy.

'I do not see any canvas Poppy, where is it and why should I want it to be blank'?

"It was just a figure of speech', Poppy replied, believing her new boss possessed an extremely dry and dusty sense of humour.

Tom thought this over. His grandmother, Mutte, sometimes used this same phrase. He realised it was something to do with the way his brain worked. Tom wondered whether he should ask his doctor about 'figures of speech'. Doctor Hari Goringe had treated him since he was six years of age. Yes, he would ask him.

Dr Goringe once told him all the parts were in his brain, but they were in the wrong order. He understood what he meant. Tom realised he thought differently to other people. There were men at work who laughed uproariously at a 'joke', but Tom did not understand the point of the story. Often the 'jokes' these days were about jews. 'They have long noses' or were 'greedy' or 'cheaters.' He knew many jews. He lived in a district where there were numerous Jewish households. Tom thought, if anything, they were nicer than most people. They did not make fun of him or laugh at his expense when he failed to understand a joke or appreciate an anecdote. His old doctor was Jewish, and he was the nicest man Tom knew. 'It is

Goringe without the 'e' after 'o' and with the 'e' after 'g' he would say. Tom did not understand what he meant until the doctor explained that he was jokingly telling people he was not related to Herman Goring the Reich Marshall. Tom did not think this was funny. He would have been surprised if he was a relative of the Reich Marshall.

'Are you a barber Poppy'? he asked.

'No, I am your personal assistant. I will get you supplies, bring you coffee and lunch and make sure your car is ready. You do not have a designated driver, but I will get one from the pool. The chief of staff has told me you will be permitted to cut cabinet minister's and senior officer's hair. We will be busy enough. Herr Himmler and General Polan have already made appointments.'

Poppy grew up in the South. Her father was the local blacksmith, and her mother took in washing and carried out chores for a few English swells who pretended to grow Riesling grapes and produced thin acidic wine that remained largely un-drunk. When the Communist extremist's bomb hit the town in 1932 Poppy aged 16 was on her bike delivering a carton of English tea to one of the swells. When she heard the thump followed by the explosion, shouts and screams she immediately knew what occurred. She dropped off the tea and refused help from the English couple at the vineyard. She rode back to the village. She knew without being told the extent of the disaster. There would be no survivors. She found her way to the nearest town with a railway station and using the money given to her for the tea she took a train to Berlin. Fortunately, Poppy looked older than her years. She found work as a chamber maid and worked for a Jewish family in the 5th Reindorsement until they hurriedly left for the USA. She met a girl in a tabac who worked as a typist. She learned the craft and was offered a job, as a junior, at the Chancelry. Her initiative and work ethic was recognised, and she was moved into clerical positions culminating in her appointment as assistant to Tom Wgner.

There was a sharp rap on the door and Heinrich Beck walked in.

'My name is Heinrich Beck; I am representing the German Union of Workers. You will be expected to join'.

Poppy was unimpressed. She looked Beck up and down with undisguised disdain.

'Do you have a permit to enter this area? It is reserved for senior officers?'

Beck was taken aback by her insolence, but he pulled a sheet of paper out from his pocket and handed it to her.

Poppy examined it carefully, folded it and handed it back to Beck.

'You are a junior employee of Herr Goebbels with only limited right of access. I suggest you consult one of the senior staff before you come barging in here making demands. Personal employees of the Fuehrer are not required to join unions'

Tom Wagner watched the exchange with interest.

'You certainly do not need a haircut. Your hair was cut this morning at Ferdia's Barber Shop. It looks very modern. It has been layered nicely'.

Heinrich Beck was confused. Was this fellow trying to take a rise out of him? And the young woman she was brazen and offensive. He would remember her.

'I will consult my superiors,' he said, leaving the salon with as much dignity as he could muster.

When the door was shut, Poppy smiled and gave a little hop.

'He is a nasty toad, but we got rid of him. You are employed by the Fuehrer himself and do not have to join his silly union. You just saw Poppy at work'.

Tom was somewhat confused, by the encounter, but thanked her for 'her guidance.'

Beck remained angry. He was convinced there was something wrong with Tom Wagner. Was he touched or worse was he an enemy agent? He heard his mother was English. Beck decided to keep an eye on Wagner. He understood he would not receive authority for such a venture. He would do it on his own time.

7

BERLIN

Tobias Fox spent some time with Masterson at the Embassy pretending to seek information about likely buyers of Islay whisky.

He carried a letter of introduction from the Islay Distillers Association. This was supplied by Oliver Lancet and was a fine forgery. He was allegedly visiting Berlin to endeavour to promote the region. He was also banging the drum for his own brand. McGonagle Malt was a fine Speyside dram that carried a tradition of good cheer. In his knapsack was a bottle of the 12-year aged single malt.

Masterson greeted him warmly.

'I seem to know your name; did you ever do some scrambling for the firm in Belfast'?

This remark would have seemed odd, perhaps unintelligible to a mere purveyor of Holy Scottish Water. Tobias decided to take a middle ground.

'I am a Scot, a Speyside man Sir. I am no Paddy whacker. I did some translating for a British crew a few years ago. I have a knack for languages. It was strictly on consignment. I never joined the firm.'

Masterson did not seem convinced, but his concerns were allayed when Tobias produced the bottle.

'With my compliments, it is a fine dram. You will get a taste of blackcurrants dark chocolate and some smoke from the Spey'.

'This is a great pleasure. The German whiskies are best used to fuel engines.'

Later over coffee, damned good coffee, at the strange little shopping street, deserted except for the café cum flower shop Tobias met the owner. She was a middle-aged attractive woman. She examined Fox with interest.

'Can I get you and your visitor tea or coffee Mr Masterson?'

She left with their orders for strong coffee and a last look of curiosity at Tobias.

'Odd accent', Tobias Fox said to Masterson.

'Mrs Wagner is an Englishwoman. She was married to a German Airman. He was killed in the Great War. She stayed on after the war. She has an adult son. He is a barber. He has just been employed by Hitler as the official Chancelry haircutter. He is a strange young fellow but is supposed to be very clever. He never smiles. The Germans have a name for it, but then again, they have a name for everything. I think they say he is autistic – whatever that means. They have doctors who are called psychiatrists. Many of them are Jewish. They are caught in a cleft stick. The Nazis say the Jews are an inferior race, but they are the best mind doctors. Many of these doctors have left Germany. Hitler is rounding up jews and placing them in special camps. He is doing the same with Gipsies. He was gathering Holy Romans, but the Pope persuaded him to ease up.

The Fuehrer was worried the Catholics were more loyal to God than him.'

Tobias took in the information but did not reply.

'Best coffee in Berlin', Masterson said, over a pleasant lunch of pates, cold meats and blinis served by the handsome woman.

'Do you have any plans for this evening. I make it my job to explore the fleshpots. There is quite a selection. I recommend The Lady Windermere. The hoi polloi, foreign correspondents, black-market merchants and rough-necks jostle.'

'Thanks for the offer but it is unlikely such a place would buy blends let alone Single Malts.'

They discussed the whisky trade and the joys of Berlin. Tobias deduced the man was a molly, and he made no attempt to either encourage or discourage him into believing he was similarly disposed. He understood why Lancet used outside help. The man was also a fool. Still his recommendation for evening entertainment was likely to be up to the minute. It was probably all he was good for.

Berlin at night was rowdy and loud. In the central Mitte area, young women dressed in fashionably short floral print dresses, walked arm in arm. Young men eyed them off. Working class boys wearing ill-fitting tweed suits and cloth caps sauntered the streets in groups. Swells in black shiny ensembles and pointy patent leather shoes minced here and there and occasionally one could hear a beating drum and a group of Nazi bovver boys, in their sinister black and brown, would march the footpaths singing lustily and casting a wake through the citizenry.

Tobias Fox held his liquor well. It was an imperative for a purveyor of whisky. He was a firm believer that the best information was the tittle-tattle passed round a bar over drinks. Alcohol loosened tongues and dispersed emotions.

He sat at the bar of The Lady Windermere, which turned out to be a downstairs hole in the wall in the Tee Bee district, not far from his hotel. He had come on a whim and the whisper from Masterson, but, he remembered, a Berlin purveyor of fake cognac once also recommended it.

'A lot of the journos, at least the degenerate ones, hang out there. Cheap liquor, boys and girls but do not touch the food'.

The bar was crowded, and every table was taken. There was a tiny stage enclosed by a curtain. A chanteuse mournfully warbled German love songs on a loudspeaker. There was one table that interested Tobias Fox. There was an odd mix of people, seven or eight of them, talking loudly and copiously drinking vodka. Dominating the table was a bulky man. His hair was black and stood stiff in an almost bouffant style. He wore a solid black suit and even his tie was mainly black but softened only slightly by some threads of white silk. His eyes moved slowly but surely around the room like searchlights attempting to find a target. He momentarily fixed on Fox who ignored the gaze, but took it in.

'Nothing sexual there', thought Tobias, 'was I a rival, a copper or a plant'?

The remainder of the table was a potpourri. There was a handsome young man. Tobias thought he was an English swell and probably a molly at that. A noisy and rumpled young woman sat next to him There were a couple of other females, hiding beer flab under diaphanous gowns, being pawed by a drunk and obnoxious German officer. There was also a handsome middle-aged woman dressed in a conservative business suit. She was coiffed with a bun. She was flanked by a voluble elderly lady and a silent young man who stared implacably at the dance floor but showed no joy at what he saw. Tobias looked again. The woman, with the bun, was the owner of the café where he dined that morning with Masterson. She was talking to the noisy young woman, who, on closer inspection was a little grubby as well as dishevelled.

Tobias Fox could not believe his luck. Only this morning he was told of the young man employed as a barber at the Chancelry and here was his mother and, most likely, the barber himself. He was considering the best way to approach the table. He understood that the man in black was the padrone.

'That is Harry Lime at the end table', said the fellow on the stool next to Tobias, 'he is the greatest black marketeer in Vienna. He must have business in Berlin'.

Tobias examined his neighbour. He was very young and had the Nazi haircut. He wore a loud check suit, no doubt, sold to him as the height of modern fashion. He bore an air of perceived haughty authority.

'Good evening', said Tobias in a formal way, 'I am Tobias Fox'.

The young fellow seemed momentarily discombobulated. 'Hello, my name is Heinrich Beck'.

'I work for Dr Goebbels', he added.

'I am a whisky vendor from Scotland. Do you like single malts?'

'I have never tasted one. I stick to Schnapps. I am a German'.

Tobias thought this latter comment was unnecessary. The young man looked like a fool, but one never knew. Perhaps a steel-trap mind was hidden by the gauche presence.

'What do you do for Dr Goebbels'? he asked, not expecting a responsive answer.

'I am a trainee intelligence officer. I work in the Chancelry'.

Tobias Fox was unsure whether the man was very smart or very stupid. Even the greenest British agents would keep their identity hidden. He remembered an Irish rogue who was described as Paddy the spy, but he was a master of double deception. Nobody could imagine a fellow advertising he was an agent could be the real thing.

'That is very impressive. I do not think I have ever met an intelligence officer before. May I enquire why you are here? Forgive me for prying, but it is quite an honour for a whisky salesman to meet an important intelligence officer'.

Tobias wondered if he had laid on the trowel a bit too thick, but Heinrich Beck, if anything, seemed quite chuffed by the compliment.

'There is a fellow over at that corner table who interests me. I do not have anything concrete to go on yet, but I have a nose for such matters.'

Heinrich gestured towards the rear table. The table where the man in black was holding court. Tobias guessed Harry Lime was the subject of the young man's interest. He was wrong.

A waiter bent down to talk to Harry Lime. He rose and walked directly over to Tobias Fox.

'Mr Lime was wondering if you would care to join his table', intoned the waiter.

Tobias nodded to Harry Lime who was looking directly towards him. He rose.

'I have been invited to join the table you are watching. Do not worry your secret is safe with me'.

He walked towards the end table. He took a last look at Beck. 'I should have told him that intelligent agents keep their mouths shut', he thought to himself as Beck's mouth was agape in surprise and confusion.

Lime rose as he approached.

'Hello, I am Harry Lime. I would like you to meet Larry Cromarty, he is our resident author, fresh from Cambridge'.

'I was sent down from Cambridge Harry, do not forget that piece of my legend'.

'For writing dirty doggerel on his exam paper', piped up the bedraggled girl, who was even more a mess close than viewed from a distance, 'but he has met Auden. I know that for a fact. I saw them together. They are both mollies but not with each other'.

'And our noisy young friend is a noted songbird also from England Ronnie Tolar'.

Harry Lime took Tobias around the table introducing him to each with an accompanying brief biography. There was a topiarist from Wellesley, wherever that was, a scientist from Bermondsey and a Captain in the German Home Guard..

'And this is Sarah Wagner, her son Tom and her mother-in-law who we affectionately call Mutte'.

'We have met', Tobias said to Sarah Wagner, 'I dined in your cafe this morning'.

Sarah Wagner nodded but showed no recognition or enthusiasm.

'And the young Nazi who was with you at the bar. I trust we are not breaking up a tryst', Tobias wondered if Harry Lime was interested in finding more about young Beck.

'I was just sitting next to him. He seems harmless enough'.

Sarah Wagner's son spoke. It seemed an effort for him.

'I know him. He works at the Chancelry. He told me he represents a union, but my assistant told me he works for Dr Goebbels. She said he mainly sorts the mail and runs his errands'.

Fox wondered if German youth had changed. The new breed seemed eager to divulge all they knew to anybody they met.

Tobias Fox found himself sitting next to Cromarty. The man was no secret agent. He was a veritable gold mine of information, Tobias guessed some was true, some was invention.

'Harry is our sinister minister,' Cromarty spoke in an urgent, camp drawl, 'he smuggles pharmaceuticals from one end of Europe to the other.'

'I doubt a black marketeer would be advertising his wares', Fox replied, 'but it makes for a fine air of mystery. Where are you from. I cannot place your accent. I am veering between Manhattan, New York and Surrey, London'.

'You are almost perfectly right. I am from Long Island and Kent. I am a writer. I travelled here following in the footsteps of Isherwood, Spender and Auden'.

Cromarty spoke of the writers Christopher Isherwood, Stephen Spender and W.H Auden as if Tobias Fox must have known of them. He knew of them but not because of their literary talent. The service kept an eye on all notorious emigres.

'I share an apartment, well more a room with Ronnie. She is a singer. You will hear her soon.'

Tobias must have raised an eyebrow because Cromarty placed a hand on his arm.

'We are not lovers. I am her confidante. I am a camera'.

'I am a whisky blender and purveyor. I am unaware of the literary world or show business. This is most exciting for me. I will have stories to tell back in the distillery in Speyside'.

He did not add the Service viewed authors and actors with suspicion. In the eyes of the boffins, they were usually either garrulous madmen or drunk lechers.

Tobias noticed that Ronnie Tolar had slipped away. The stage at the end of the room was enclosed with a heavy and soiled damask curtain. The drink steward lifted the hatch at the end of the bar and pulled the curtain open. The rear stage door opened and a diminutive man with sparkling eyes emerged. He wore a black velvet dinner jacket and black pants with a broad red stripe that could have been owned by a dwarf guardsman. Incongruously he wore a black peaked cap. 'Mein Fraulein and Mein Herren it is my honour to introduce you to the great English vocalist. She is the rose of Covent Garden and the lily of Piccadilly. I give you Ronnie Tolar'.

He opened the door and an elderly woman with a formidable bodice took up her position at a piano in the corner of the stage. She was followed by a bushy haired trumpeter and lastly came Ronnie. She was transformed. She wore a shimmering white gown with a slit that displayed a shapely leg encased in black silk. Her lips were crimson, and her hair was transformed into a lustrous curlicue. She sang in a husky contralto, not always catching the note, but with such conviction the crowd was, none-the-less, captured by her sultry chic.

The piano player played a rhythm and bass with her left hand, leaving her right hand to occasionally flourish a chord while the saxophonist blew a woolly sound that matched his hirsute appearance

The Harry Lime table had turned their chairs to face the stage and their thunderous applause at the end of each song dared the rest of the crowd to not follow suit.

Ronnie Tolar finished her set and exited the stage. She was replaced by a clarinettist and a kettle drummer.

Tobias Fox noticed that Heinrich Beck left. He threw some marks on the bar and with a last glance towards the end table strode to the door. Tobias met his eyes for a moment before turning towards Harry Lime. The big man smiled back, in what seemed to Tobias, to be a conspiratorial way.

Fox pulled his chair across to be next to Sarah Wagner.

'It is indeed a coincidence to run into you here on the same day we met at your beautiful shop'.

Tobias was no lady's man. He never married, was not a father and his family had mainly been his brothers. Sure, there were parents, but they died from an excessive intake of the very spirit that he now distilled to sell to others. His brothers were cut from different cloth. They partook of the juice of the barley but worked the long hours and lifted the heavy cartons necessary to run the business. They looked out for Tobias when he was home working the still. Tobias had the gift, the mixing gift that made the juice of the barley turn from a pleasant amber drink to a tiny touch of magic.

Sarah seemed amused by his interest.

'This is not a place that I visit regularly. Ronnie once worked for me. She is a beautiful spirit and a talented singer, but this place is a little raffish for me'.

'Raffish', Tobias thought of the word. It was not used often. He had seen it in books. His spy's mind was operating. Sarah was probably starved of English-speaking friends. 'Raffish' was a word found in books, Victorian romances where the villain was a 'raffish fellow. He gathered his thoughts and slipped back to the present.

'Is tonight a special occasion'? he asked.

'Oh yes', she answered, 'my son has secured a job in the Chancelry. He is a barber. He is to be the personal hairdresser to the Cabinet. He expects even cut the Fuehrer's hair occasionally when his regular barber is unavailable.'

'I saw the article in the paper. I did not connect you with the barber. I hope your boy does not become nervous. I have heard Hitler has a terrible temper. A cut on the ear would not be received well'.

'That is exactly what his old boss Ferdie said, but there is no chance of that. My son has a disability. He is devoid of emotion. He never smiles, laughs or cries but his concentration on a task is excellent. We have taken him to a doctor, and he has told us my son has a condition the mind doctors call autism'.

'You have a husband'? asked Tobias.

'A husband, no, why do you ask'?

'You said 'we' went to the mind doctor'.

'My! You are observant. No, I live with my mother-in-law. My husband was a pilot. He died in the Great War. Did you serve'?

Tobias thought this over. He was not sure of the politics of the woman. She sounded as British as anybody strap-hanging on the Clapham Omnibus, but she married a Kraut and continued to live in Berlin years after the war was over. Her reference to Hitler was neutral. Tobias answered accordingly.

'I was ground staff, ordinance, pen pushing that kind of thing'.

'Looks can be deceiving', she replied, 'I would have pegged you as an infantry man.'

The music stopped, the curtain closed, and the lights in the restaurant brightened. Chairs were pushed back and around the room conversation commenced and glasses tinkled. Soon enough Sarah, her son and the older woman rose.

'Tom has an early start, it is time for us to go home', she said.

'We could share a cab', said Larry Cromarty, the camp writer.

'We travel in style. Tom has a driver'. Sarah replied.

Tobias waved her goodbye.

'Ronnie has found a German lover so I will stay and drink with Harry Lime'. Cromarty said, 'he can fill me in about the fleshpots of Vienna, if there are any amongst the schnitzel palaces and bratwurst bars.'

Tobias was vaguely and strangely jealous of the carefree and strangely intimate exchange, but surely the man was a molly.

The other members of the party drifted off leaving Harry Lime, Cromarty and Tobias.

'It seems you have made an impression on our beautiful widow', said Harry Lime, 'unfortunately she is watched over like a woodland kite by her mother-in-law and has a son to care for'.

'She seems a very nice woman', said Tobias in a neutral way.

'That bloody boy is a handful. Apparently, there is no cure', said Cromarty.

'What actually is wrong with him'?

'The Viennese mind doctors call it autism. He demonstrates no feelings. They called it a closed brain disability', interposed Harry Lime.

'Is there no cure? He seems to be physically sound, and he has a very responsible occupation'? asked Tobias.

'The Nazi butchers claim an operation will cure the disease. I read a report that madman Dr Merz posits that by shifting brain lobes around the brain he can cure diseases of the mind. He mentioned autism. He also said homosexuality could be cured by inverting the frontal lobe of the brain', Cromarty said.

'When is your operation being performed? asked Harry Lime.

'As Charles Dickens would say when the moon turns to blue cheese', Cromarty replied.

After another round of drinks, the trio said their goodbyes. Harry Lime offered to share a cab with Tobias. When they arrived at his hotel and as Tobias Fox was alighting Harry Lime leant across the seat and spoke.

'If you are ever in Vienna, make sure and stay at the Hotel Glock. Frau Glock is an old friend. Do not forget to mention my name'.

'I doubt if I will be going to Vienna Harry', Tobias replied.

'One never knows', said Harry and the taxi sped off.

8

LONDON

Oliver Lancet read Tobias Fox's report of his visit to The Lady Windermere. The name Harry Lime was well known to him. The man was an enigma. On one hand he provided the Service with occasional shards of valuable information about German agents of influence in London. On the other hand, there was guff in the corridors that he was a source of Nazi intelligence about English ship movements and Embassy shenanigans. Rumour also swirled he was a smuggler, though the contraband was never identified. Was he a black-market weapons peddler or was information his only stock in trade?

He read Tobias report of his contact with the Wagner family. If it had been anybody else, but Tobias Fox, Oliver Lancet would have been suspicious. Honey pots were a common or garden tool in the espionage world, but they would not work with Tobias Fox. He was no lady's man. His bluff demeanour and grizzled exterior were not conducive to the art of seduction. Nevertheless, there were shards of glitter veiled in the dross. Young Tom Wagner was in a unique position. He would be cutting Cabinet Minister's hair. It was unlikely he would be privy to state secrets, but proximity bred familiarity. He was a catch.

Oliver wondered about the Wagner family. The widow was English, but she married a Hun, a famous brave one, but still a Hun. Lancet remembered the woman. She served him coffee. She was friendly enough and the coffee was damned good, but he had no opportunity to form a view as to her loyalties. He picked up his phone and spoke to his secretary.

'Get me Parrott'.

Soon enough the fellow arrived. Lancet sometimes wondered about his name. Was Parrott his surname, or simply a sobriquet. He looked like a bird, what with his spiky tawny hair, his thin fingers and pointy shoes. His clothes complemented the name. Parrott, today, was wearing a Glen Plaid jacket, a mottled hairy sweater and odd narrow waisted black pants. Even the man's speech was reminiscent of a bird. He squeaked rather than talked. Whatever his appearance he was the Cage's best burrower. If there was anything to find he would root it out.

Parrott sat at the very edge of his chair waiting for instructions.

'There is a woman in Berlin by the name of Sarah Wagner. She is English by birth but was married to a German airman. He was killed in the Great War, but she continues to live in Berlin with her son and mother-in-law. I want you to compile a dossier on the family, particularly the woman. I want your work to be totally undercover. Do not go to the Embassy. Use public records wherever possible. I want the information as soon as possible. Here is an expenses chit. You will need to go to Berlin. Make that your first stop. Reverse engineer. Find the lady's antecedents.'

Parrott seemed pleased to be offered the task. He wrote furiously into a large notebook with a thick black pencil. He left happily squeaking to himself.

Parrott bagged a flight to Berlin. His chit got him a first-class seat. The flight steward was unimpressed by his sole premium passenger. His order of a cup of weak tea and a digestive biscuit did not help. It was not the usual fare requested by his customers.

On the day after his arrival Parrott scoured the records at the Berlin Public Administration office. He had no time for the fleshpots, and he returned to London on a tramp steamer that evening. Masterson, at the Embassy, saw the copy visa. He wondered if Oliver Lancet was bypassing him.

'Surely not, they were both, after all, Oxford men.'

The marriage records were readily available. The Germans compliled, filed and recorded with Teutonic efficiency. Sarah Wagner was listed in the Marriage Certificate as Sarah Green, a spinster from Whitechapel in London. There was no London address or occupation given. At the Public Library he found newspaper records of the nuptials. They focussed on Herr Wagner who was a serious war hero. There was a grainy print in the weekly women's section that Parrott photographed. Upon his return to London, he spent a day at the British Public Library and later made enquiries from a book worm at the Cage.

He did not find a Sarah Green that fitted the description, but there was a Sarah Greengrass of approximately the correct age who came from

Whitechapel. Parrott found a Thomas Greengrass with an address in Lyme Passage.

Whitechapel was windswept and gloomy by day. The solemn grey stone buildings and the narrow-cobbled laneways cast a grey pall even when the sun shined bright, which was rarely enough. The sound of footsteps in the passageways was magnified and reverberated against the stone walls. Tours of Jack the Ripper's working environment were popular. There was no need for any stage props. The place was haunting, if not haunted. Parrott noticed none of this.

Lyme Passage was an alley that ran between Aldershot Road and Mene Street. It was lined with Victorian Terraces and an occasional ancient timber shack awaiting demolition. There was the odd sign in windows advertising a room to let, often with the added words 'share bath'. Parrot barely noticed the environs as he tracked his quarry He rapped on the door of a two-story terrace. The door was answered by a large, puffy woman who was probably younger than she looked. She did not seem to be pleased to see Parrott.

'What are you selling? Whatever it is I don't want any.', she was wearing a shapeless bundle of wool that was probably a dressing gown. She carried a broom, and an onlooker may have wondered if she could use it to fly away.

'I am looking for a lady', Parrott said.

'You have come to the wrong place. Those days are over. Go to Soho'.

'No, I am looking to find the relatives of a lady named Sarah Green. It is nothing nefarious, I assure you! I am with a firm of solicitors. A relative has died. She may be entitled to an annuity.'

'It sounds very suspicious', the woman replied, still leaning on the broom but showing no sign of ending the conversation.

'I am Sarah Greengrass, but I have never been known as Green. Why should I lop a bit off my name. My family have always lived in this street. We also have a few relatives in Greek Street. We are one of the most famous cockney families in London. There are also Greengrass's who travel as Pikeys. They are not as well thought of'.

She stopped short waiting for a reaction from Parrott.

'I am sure you come from fine stock madam, but do you know of a young woman about your age whose name is Sarah Green'.

'Young woman, that is a laugh. I am old as God's dog and never found a man. There was a Sarah at the elementary school, but she was no Green. She was a kike. She was the daughter of the tailor on the High Street. The firm was Rosenberg and Greenbaum. She was a Greenbaum'.

'And she didn't shorten her name'?

'It would have done no good. We all knew who she was. She was uppity for a yid's daughter. I heard the mother was a drunk and a slut. The girl did not stay long in the Chapel. The gossip was she went off to Europe. She had relatives on the continent. The tailor's shop is long gone. Somebody told me the father retired and went to Cheam. He ran the business on his own. There never was a Rosenberg. She would be left money, wouldn't she. My bloody rellos are pikeys in Kent. They only own what they steal. My rent is controlled and my dad left me a little poultice. He was a rag and bone man and a good one at that'.

Parrott listened patiently. Sarah Greengrass eventually ran out of patter and steam.

'If you hear anything or remember something, could you give me a call. I will leave my number.' Parrott wrote a phone number on a sheet of pad that he took from his top pocket.

Parrott's next stop was Cheam. He took the train. He found the police station and presented his credentials. The desk jockey looked him up and down with some disfavour, but after a talk to his sergeant and a call to London he was taken to the sergeant's office.

'I am looking for a Mr Greenbaum. He would be old. He was a tailor in Whitechapel, but I doubt he would still be working. He may be dead'.

'I knew the man and he is long dead and buried. You will find him in the graveyard. He was no Anglican, but he used to play chess with the vicar, who made an exception and laid him to rest in the church yard.'

'Did he have any relatives?'

'The vicar told me he had a daughter, but she was living abroad. He was a testy chap. He probably fell out with her. The vicar was his only friend and if it was not for the chess he may have been friendless'.

Parrott heard enough. He returned to London and presented his report to Oliver Lancet.

9
SCOTLAND

Tobias Fox was back at the distillery working his magic on the juice of the barley. His brothers were glad he had returned.

He could not help but think of his last few days in Berlin. He spent two more evenings at The Lady Windermere. Larry Cromarty was ever present, and the girl Ronnie Tolar sang her sultry ballads and bewitched lumpish Bavarian businessmen with her coquetry and husky voice. There were others at the table, but they came and went. There was no sign of the Wagner family. Fox did not mention them and their friend Ronnie did not raise the subject. Harry Lime was absent, but his spirit was ever present.

The brothers back in Scotland were getting restless and Tobias rang The Cage.

'Oliver, I need to go home. I have made a valuable contact, more valuable than expected but Tom Wagner must be given a chance to settle into his new job. My brothers need me back at the distillery.'

'You still do not know whether the boy will co-operate. For all we know he may be a dedicated Nazi.

I suggest before you leave you partake of a fine cup of coffee. Renew your cordial acquaintance with the widow'.

Tobias was not surprised by Lancet's apparent knowledge of Sarah's business nor his veiled, unspoken suggestion he may hanker for Frau Wagner. Oliver Lancet was a human puppeteer and a master of subtlety.

Fox booked a commercial flight home using his Cage travel stipend. The flight was to leave on the following morning. He took a cab to the Blutenblatt. He arrived in mid-morning. Sarah Wagner was, in the window, arranging a large bowl of tulips as a display. There were no other customers and Tobias stood near the window and chatted with Sarah.

'How is young Tom liking his new position? It certainly is a step upwards. He will be a celebrity hair cutter. His future is assured'.

There was a fair amount of hyperbole in this statement. Tobias was not normally phased or disquieted. Somehow Sarah unsettled him. Tobias had never been a ladies' man. Sure, there were brief encounters and the occasional minor entanglement. They never lasted. The woman would tire of Tobias. He was never one for small talk. He knew nothing of what a woman would want. He was most at home in a warm bar, with a crackling peat fire burning, a dram of fine single malt and the company of hardy lowlanders. They would discuss the quality of the Pedro Ximenez casks or the new copper still installed at Benrannach. Occasionally a man may mention a wife or daughter, but only to highlight an anecdote or a grumble.

Sarah lowered herself from the window ledge and gestured Tobias to a seat.

'I have a brew ready I will get you a cup. My mother-in-law has made Lebkuchen. They are supposed to be a Christmas treat, but Mutte prepares a batch regularly'.

Sarah joined Tobias with the coffee and treats.

'I am going back to Scotland tomorrow'. He paused. He realised he sounded stilted and awkward. 'I was going to see if you would enjoy dinner with me. Perhaps it can wait until I come back. I have made some valuable contacts. There is even talk of production of a German style whisky with less peat smoke and more cherry flavour'.

Oliver ceased speaking. He felt a little foolish. Sarah laid a hand on his arm.

'Would you like to come home for dinner this evening. It will be simple, but Mutte's beef dumplings are special'.

After a day of visiting liquor merchants Tobias Fox found himself seated in the cozy front room at the back of the Wagner home sipping a, surprisingly good, German sherry and chatting with Sarah and Tom. Mutte could be heard clattering away in the kitchen preparing the dumplings.

'How is your new job?' asked Tobias of Tom Wagner.

'I like having a car to take me to work. Poppy makes me coffee. She waits for me to arrive and she stores my luncheon sandwich in a pantry. I shave Herr Hitler every morning and trim his moustache. He sometimes gets me to crop his fringe. His hair is thinning, and I layer the combover. He is a difficult client as he talks the whole time. His staff walk in and out. When I finish with Herr Hitler I see other men by appointment. Herr Himmler is not very nice, and Herr Goebbels is very quiet. Some of the generals are pleasant. General Jurgen Hoeven is very friendly. He speaks English to me. He says he is practising conversing in a foreign tongue. The only man who is very rude to me is a fellow called Heinrich Beck. He works for Dr Goebbels. He has the modern short back and sides with a coif. Poppy sends him away. She says he is a Schizakopf.'

'Heinrich Beck', Tobias remembered the gauche young Nazi from the bar at the Lady Windermere. Apparently, he was still on the prowl.

Tom seemed to have exhausted his description of his work environment. He sat back in his seat and began fiddling with his hands, pressing his thumbs together and waggling his fingers.

'It sounds like Tom has a very loyal assistant in Poppy', said Tobias.

'A very pretty assistant', Sarah replied, 'she came here one day to drop off a new manicure set.'

Young Tom's fingers twirled faster, and he began looking down at his feet.

'It is all right, Tom, do not be embarrassed', said Sarah.

After a fine meal washed down with a bottle of Alsace-Lorraine Shiraz Tobias took a cab back to his hotel.

As planned, he returned to Scotland, but his mind kept returning to Sarah Wagner. He was drawn to her, as a moth to a flickering light. He felt compelled to soon return to Berlin.

'I have many new contacts,' he told his brothers. 'There is an untapped market for our single malts.

The new military class dines and entertains lavishly. Our whisky is more succulent than the German drams. The other Speyside distillers are not aware of the new market. We should steal a march on them.'

He told Lancet a different tale.

'I need to gain the confidence of the Wagner family. The son likes me, but I need to gain the trust of his mother and grandmother.'

His brothers bought the story. Lancet was not so sure. Tobias reminded him of a racehorse his family once owned. The mare pulled and struggled as it was led to the starting stalls. It bit attendants, tried to throw jockeys and lashed the wire cage with her hooves. Then the race commenced, and the horse ran like the wind. It won four races until it pulled up lame at Epsom. 'Trying too hard,' the trainer commented. This was Tobias. He was difficult to get to the barrier but was a fine exponent of the dark art of espionage once he commenced his op. Lancet was prepared to watch and wait. 'Perhaps Tobias has found mid-life ambition.'

Tobias flew commercial. During the three weeks after he returned to Berlin he saw Sarah Wagner every day. He often ate at the family apartment, usually bringing treats for Tom. He found some Alfred Dunhill shaving soap and badger hairbrushes. Tom opened the package carefully and swayed from side to side with pleasure.

The family picnicked with Tobias in the Tiergarten, and he even took Tom fishing. 'It's a man's sport,' he told Sarah when she hinted, she would like to go.

Finally, and with great encouragement from Mutte, he took Sarah to dinner. They ate at the new French restaurant in Kurfstendamm. Tobias did not profess his love. He did not need to. They held hands at the table and later without a word being spoken Sarah accompanied him to his hotel. They made love. It was awkward. They were both shy, even diffident. Later Tobias escorted her home. They kissed in the taxi like old lovers and arranged to meet the next day.

Tobias spent the next three weeks in Berlin. It felt to him like a dream. Mutte was a conspirator. She encouraged them, making slightly suggestive comments and patting Tobias on the arm as she passed with food or wine. Young Tom seemed at ease with Tobias and often spoke of his customers, equipment and even the new styles that were being featured in American magazines.

Finally, Tobias had to go home to Scotland. His brothers were almost frantic.

'We need a new batch. You are our master distiller.'

'I will return as soon as I can,' he told Sarah, 'I have never felt like this before.'

He thought of himself as a brave Scotchman but now was tongue-tied with fear. Finally, he gathered himself.

'I love you Sarah,' he said.

'I know,' she replied, 'I feel the same.'

After his return to Scotland Tobias was unsurprised to find Oliver Lancet on his doorstep. The two men walked the dales.

Tobias was careful to only talk of the Wagner family in a detached manner.

Lancet was his usual careful self, but when Tobias Fox finished his de-brief he said, 'well done Tobias, but you know you will have to go back. Churchill is insistent. The barber is a great stroke of luck and more than luck, very good management. There are a few loose ends I first need to clear up. Book a flight next week. In the meantime, blend your whisky, quaff a dram or two, get back in your brothers' good graces'.

The two men returned to the distillery and without so much as a by-your-leave Lancet was ushered into the back seat of a black Humber Snipe and driven away.

10

LONDON - BERLIN

On his way back to the Cage Oliver Lancet began to assemble the parts. The young barber's appointment may be a huge stroke of luck, but then again, the fellow was brought up as a German, and his father is a dead war hero. He is hardly likely, under these circumstances, to have warm feelings towards the English. The allies probably shot down his father. He was, also, not sure where the young barber's disability fitted into the picture. Oliver had a healthy obloquy towards the new fad of mental illness. Hell, if you wash your hands too often you have a ritualistic disorder according to the mind benders. It sounded like hocus-pocus to Lancet. He decided to speak to the Cage newly minted honorary psychiatrist when he returned to London.

As Lancet pondered Fox's legend of the young barber's life in the Chancelry he recalled General Jurgen Hoeven. He is the sleeper, or is he? 'Is he still onboard?' And there is Harry Lime. 'Everybody knows Harry Lime, but whose side is he on?'

On the following morning Oliver Lancet sat in the Harley Street rooms of the Cage consultant psychiatrist.

Dr Bella Varrenna was an Italian who trained in Rome under disciples of Freud. She was a tall and angular. She stooped, probably to diminish her height, Dr Varenna was in her middle years but dressed in a swirling silk flowery patterned low bodice skirt favoured by young cognoscenti.

'Closed in personality, autism, oh yes, I know of the illness well. There is no cure. The disease can be managed. However, one must be sensitive. These patients live on a knife edge'.

'Doctor we are on the verge of another war. I am interested in recruiting a person with this illness to carry out a dangerous but not a violent task. If his mental health is deleteriously affected so be it. In wars there are casualties. I hope you understand. I do not want a treatment schedule I want to simply understand how to trigger the man to obey instructions. I want him motivated.'

The doctor sighed.

'I know the terms of my employment Mr Lancet. I was simply explaining the consequences of imprudent action. A person suffering from autism usually has one authority figure. This person exercises control. The patient can be directed by the authority figure. There is a limit to this control. A sufferer has only marginal control over their mental function. It, of course, depends on the extent of the disability. If the person can hold a job or develop a relationship the disability is relatively minor. Often there is lability. The patient may have ups and downs.'

Lancet returned to the Cage and re-read Parrott's report. He knew his next task was unpleasant, but he was used to unpleasant tasks.

On the following morning, he left for Berlin.

He booked into a hotel well away from the British Embassy. The next morning after nibbling the usual cold cut breakfast provided in two-star German hotels, he phoned the Bluttenblatt Café and Flower Shop.

'My name is Oliver Lancet, Mrs Wagner,' he said, 'we have not formally met but I need to see you urgently. It concerns your son.'

Lancet gave nothing away. He did not need to. His voice carried weight. His words dripped with the resonance of power and authority.

'Can you come here?'

'No Mrs Wagner, that is not convenient. I suggest the restaurant at the Northern edge of the Tiergarten. You close at 5.00pm. Make it 6pm. The park and restaurant will be crowded. I will be seated and will stand and welcome you.'

Oliver Lancet did not wait for an answer and hung up.

Sarah Wagner spent the day worrying. Tom had left for work bright and early. He seemed to have struck up a friendship with his assistant. 'What is her name, oh that's right, it is Poppy. That surely cannot be her real name and Poppies are pretty enough, but they are common and humble, why call yourself Poppy, why not Gardenia or even Lily'. Unfortunately, there were few customers and the day dragged. She closed a little early and caught the U-Bahn to Tiergarten. The man had been correct. The park was teeming with people. Young couples were cooing hand in hand as they slowly took the by-ways, old fellows in gaberdine fed the ducks in the central pond, business types used the park as a short cut and tourists with box cameras snapped the swans and squirrels. She arrived at the busy café. She saw and recognised Lancet before he saw her. A middle-aged English gentleman, in an elegant, tailored suit stood out among the ill cut flannel of the men and over ripe colourful dresses of the women. He rose and waved. She sat down opposite him and waited. It was an unusual experience for Sarah to be wary of her company. Usually, the opposite applied. Sarah Wagner was used to living among people who were suspicious of her. If it was not for her late husband's fame she would be barely tolerated or shunned. Even the Juden who were generally amenable were wary of her, but they were now naturally suspicious of everybody.

'We have been keeping an eye on your son. He has found himself lodged in a unique niche'.

'We! Mr Lancet?'

'I am not going to identify my agency. I could give you a card. I have a dozen, but it would mean nothing. I suppose it is possible I could be a German spion, but it is unlikely. They are cut from coarser cloth.'

Lancet was impressed by her silence, her steady gaze and calm demeanour. In other circumstances she would be a fine recruit.

'What do you want from me'?

Oliver Lancet sipped his drink. It was hot chocolate. He summonsed a waiter, but Sarah shook her head, and Lancet waved the man away.

'We are concerned that Hitler is preparing to start a new world war. He claims he is interested only in peace, but certain sections of our government think otherwise'.

Sarah Wagner laughed, 'certain sections, you mean the warmongers. Fortunately, they are out of power. Stanley Baldwin is your Prime Minister. He seems to be a reasonable man'.

'This is not a time for reasonable men Mrs Wagner. Can you not observe what is happening to your Jews'. He pointed to a table of four well-dressed men who each had a yellow star of David armband.

'I understand. The government is unfair. Life is unfair. Those men are forced to wear armbands because they are Juden.'

'And so should you and so should your son Tom', Oliver Lancet replied. She said nothing but looked around a little nervously. Oliver continued.

'We have traced your provenance. I sent a man to Whitechapel. We have spoken to your neighbours. We found the old tailor shop, Rosenberg and Greenbaum. It was a good business. Not Saville Row mind you, but your father was a skilled cutter, shaper and patternmaker. You should be proud'.

'What do you want from me'.

'Well, that is the rub, you see, Mrs Wagner. We want everything and nothing. Encourage the young man to speak to you of his work, whose hair he cuts, the comings and goings. It may mean he does nothing for us, but it may mean he copies a document or remembers a conversation. You can rest assured we will look after you both. Your husband's mother is she a Nazi?'

'Far from it. She is dangerously outspoken. She has many Jewish friends.'

'I understand your lad has made a friend. Get him to bring Poppy to your home for dinner. See if she can be trusted'.

'I am not trained in the dark arts Mr Lancet', she replied.

'Mrs Wagner I would employ you in a New York minute, as the sailors say. You have already met my agent. I understand you have struck up a friendship. Tobias Fox will be back soon. You can trust him implicitly. I suppose it is possible that young Tom may hear something that I should know. I will leave you a number. I do not expect you to encourage the lad to keep an eye out – nothing like that Mrs Wagner. Keep me informed. I will leave you, my number. I will meet you within a day. Your only task for now is to assess Poppy. Contact me when you have reached a conclusion.'

Sarah drew in a breath but was able to retain her outward calm. 'Tobias is a British agent,' she reflected to herself, 'how wrong was I in trusting him. And poor Tom he adores the man, even Mutte has been bewitched.' Yet she needed to remain calm. The odds were too high. She had to protect her boy.

Oliver Lancet was gone. He left a card and money on the table and glided away. Sarah realised she hardly registered his departure. She left, but pocketed the card. She was gripped by fear for her son and anger towards Tobias. 'How could I have been so foolish.'

Poppy was excited to be invited to dinner at the Wagner's home. The invitation was delivered in an awkward way, but she was used to Tom.

'My mother wants me to ask you to dinner tomorrow', Tom said during a break from cutting the hair of some general staff members. Poppy was not disconcerted by the odd way her invitation was couched. It was just Tom being Tom.

On the following evening Poppy sat on a comfortable couch in the Wagner sitting room drinking Riesling and chatting with Sarah Wagner. Tom sat next to her. He fiddled with his fingers and looked around the room until he focussed on a piece of bric-a-brac or a photo.

'Have you always lived in Berlin Poppy', asked Sarah Wagner.

'No, I have no parents. I was born in the South', Poppy realised this sounded strange. Everybody had parents, but these were strange times.

Sarah did not seem to be surprised or compelled to question the statement.

'Tom has told me you are billeted in the Chancelry. I hope you are provided with decent accommodation and food'.

'I share with another girl, but she is never there. She enjoys entertaining junior officers. The food is good. I sometimes cook but I can get leftovers from the Chancelry kitchen. The Cabinet do not spare themselves. I particularly look forward to my dinner if Marshall Goring has hosted a lunch'.

The conversation meandered from a discussion of the latest lady's fashions and hair styles, but Sarah Wagner did not find an opportunity to discuss Poppy's politics. The meal was pleasant. Mutte was more restrained then usual. Sarah warned her to be, if not diplomatic, that would be an impossibility, at least civil towards Hitler and his gang.

'The girl may be a Nazi. Do you want your grandson to be cutting Gipsies hair in Duisburg?'

Poor Tom played little part in the discussion. He only became voluble when discussing the new fringe hairstyle for young women. Sarah noticed Poppy was solicitous and patient with him, bringing him out carefully.

Sarah, Mutte and Tom were seeing Poppy into a taxi when a group of black shirts marched past. They hesitated when they saw Poppy and the Wagner family. One of them, a gormless boy who was the son of a neighbour, whispered to his friends and they stood to attention and saluted Tom. 'Heil Hitler' they shouted before continuing their march. 'Foul swine', said Poppy quietly and Mutte hugged her warmly.

'I believe the girl can be trusted', Sarah later told Oliver Lancet over, his usual, hot chocolate at the Tiergarten. 'She has no love for the Nazis'.

'I will be in touch', said Oliver, 'just go about your life as if you had never met me'.

'I wish I had never met you', Sarah replied.

11

LONDON – BERLIN - LONDON

'I am becoming restless', said Winston Churchill. Though it was midday he was dressed in pyjamas and a silk robe. He was seated on a stool by an open fire toasting a slice of sultana bread that was skewered on the end of a long fork. Churchill's ample posterior hung over the sides of the stool as he dexterously wielded the fork. There was the inevitable glass of Scotch resting on a side table.

'I think it is likely the barber will be pliant. He is carefully controlled by his mother. I have consulted a mind doctor, and she has pointed out that people suffering from autism are often unable to control their thought and speech'.

'She', Churchill said, 'you have consulted a woman psychiatrist. Has she cured herself of female illogicality'.

'We are entering a new age, Winston. There are many women scientists and medical experts. Madame Curie and Florence Nightingale are but two examples.'

'Why not add Boadicea and Joan of Arc? Exceptions do not prove the rule'.

The old man huffed and puffed for a while.

'Tread carefully Lancet, but time will eventually run out. I am not sure which country will be the first victim. Hitler is not the Kaiser. His war will be fought around the globe. That clown Mussolini is being courted to join him, and my guess is the Fuehrer, as he calls himself, is wooing Japan. They need trade routes in the Pacific. The Dutch East Indies are at risk. Even our outposts in the Pacific, Australia and New Zealand, may be overrun. Their governments take us for granted and will expect the British Army to save them if the Japs threaten to invade. Bad luck for them, it is a pity, their fighting men were as brave as any in the Great War despite their foolish officers. It also seems the Australian politicians are as craven as ours.'

'This is far above my pay grade Winston. I hear what you say. We have a source close to the Barber. I will see what I can do'.

'Your German General'? asked Churchill.

'What German General'? Oliver lancet replied, before returning to the Cage.

While Oliver Lancet carefully defended his wicket from a Churchill googly Tom Wagner spent a quiet day in the Hair Salon. The officers were on bivouac, and Hitler and the rest of the cabinet were in the North of the country meeting and greeting functionaries. The only staff left in the Chancelry were public servants and a few bureaucrat officers.

Poppy was not pleased to see a newly minted Lieutenant Heinrich Beck walk into the main salon without so much as a by-your-leave.

'I am conducting an inventory on behalf of Dr Goebbels. I want to see your equipment Wagner.

Bring over your utensils and potions', he said to Tom who was sitting in the barber's chair reading an American hair styling magazine Poppy answered for him.

'Fuck off Beck. We are civilians. You have no authority over Tom. I will send a note to the Fuehrer's Private Secretary. Tom cuts his hair'.

Heinrich Beck turned to Tom.

'You have some strange friends Wagner. Harry Lime is a well-known black-marketeer, and his friend Larry Cromarty is a degenerate. You are judged by the company you keep. The frau Ronnie Tolar is a nutte, perhaps she lets you coite her for free'.

Tom looked blankly at Beck. He was confused by his remarks.

'I am surprised you say my friend Larry Cromarty is a degenerate. I am not sure what you mean. I have found him to be a perfect gentleman. It is true Ronnie sells her body, but she enjoys luxuries. She told me her bath soap is made with geranium petals, and she drinks champagne from a shoe as she bathes. I have not bathed with her. We have talked at The Lady Windermere. She is very amusing'.

Poppy took this in. She viewed Tom in a new light. The Lady Windermere was well known as a hang-out for all manner of vagabonds and it was rumoured sex was for sale or rent. Still, Tom's reply was seemingly innocent, if somewhat odd, but he was somewhat odd. It was part of what she liked about him.

'And I suppose Harry Lime is a simple flower seller', continued the blundering Heinrich Beck.

'No Harry Lime told me he is a man of mystery. I was not sure what he meant. I do not think he is a flower seller. My mother is a flower seller. She makes beautiful floral arrangements. Even the French Embassy buys her decorative bouquets'.

Heinrich Beck was not disarmed. He was not clever enough to have that depth of emotion. He was more just plain lost for words. 'You are an einfaltspincel', he said and walked out in disgust.

'What is an einfaltspincel Poppy, I do not know the word'? Tom asked.

'He calls you, what he is – a simpleton. You are far from that Tom. You are a man of grace and art. Your simplicity is your laurel wreath'.

She walked over to the chair and hugged Tom. He had been hugged before. Mutte often hugged him as he left for work, but not like this.

There was a rap on the door and Poppy broke away. General Jurgen Hoeven, a regular client, walked in.

'Can you fit me in for a short back and sides'? he asked in his unaccented English.

Tom rose and offered the chair.

'Do you mind if I practise my English as usual', said the General, 'I do not want to offend you ma'am' he said in German to Poppy.

'I speak some English General and thank you for your consideration', Poppy replied in English.

'Your father was an acquaintance of mine Herr Wagner. He was a fine man, a gentleman and a brave one at that'.

Tom was speechless. Most of the generals he crimped were either arrogant bullies or carried themselves with a hauteur born of a lifetime of privilege. Poppy took up the slack.

'You have very fine hair General', she said, 'Tom has made up a tonic that will feed the strands. Show General Hoeven the tonic, Tom'.

Tom opened the small jar and let the General take in its fresh aroma.

'Excellent young Tom', the General said, 'of course you can apply it. My hair needs all the help it can get'.

After General Hoeven left he sent a cable in German addressed to a nephew in Dresden.

'Congratulations on your win in the bicycle race. I look forward to attending your next meeting'.

The cable was re-forwarded to a Post Box in Guernsey. It was translated and a birthday card was posted to London where it was delivered, express post, to Oliver Lancet.

General Jurgen Hoeven had no difficulty attaching himself to the German Trade Mission to London. Hitler was still humouring Baldwin. The British Prime Minister, thereby, kept the baying hounds in Parliament on a short leash.

'We are expecting to enter a valuable agreement to trade reciprocally with Berlin. Germany is an ally we must not forget that'.

Winston Churchill, sitting in bed with a traditional English breakfast fry up plate on a tray, read the Times report of Baldwin's statement to the House with anger.

'That fool Baldwin is leading us into War', he said to nobody.

Oliver Lancet was busy entertaining the visiting German Trade allegation. It took little or no subterfuge to arrange a trout fishing excursion with General Jurgen Hoeven.

The two men drove to the Lake District and waded into a stream where they threw out their lines.

'I like the young barber', said the General, 'but I saw no sign of a rebellious nature. He is a passive young fellow. It may be his infirmity. He certainly knows his trade. He is a dexterous barber. His assistant, a young woman named Poppy, seemed more of a subversive than him. One of Goebbel's gangster boys has been trying to get her fired. He has complained that she was rude to him. The girl lives in the Chancelry Hostel and is very well liked by the matron. She has a good deal more clout than Goebbel's idiot'.

'Winston needs proof that England is a target. I am reluctant to involve you. If a war commences you will be very important to us.'

'I am not privy to Hitler's inner sanctum. My province is Military History. I teach subalterns about the great and glorious German triumphs. There are rumours, many rumours. Some say he wants to conquer France. Others talk of Eastern Europe. For all I know he wants world domination. The man is quite mad'.

'There are many civilised Germans, Jurgen. I am at a loss how they tolerate the man. He looks deranged and his speeches are so fanatical they are almost parodies. Then there are the Jews. Your country is persecuting a whole race of people. I do not understand. Are your countrymen hypnotised?'

'Humans have a history of lemming like behaviour Oliver. Remember I am an historian. The Romans became fat and complacent, the Greeks showed little appetite for hard work, they have not changed. More recently the Turks sacrificed their fourteen-hundred-year empire for what?'

'Keep an eye out for the boy. If we somehow, find a way to activate him I may need your help. I hope it does not come to that. I still want you taking up a chair at Magdalen College, Oxford one day – after the War.'

'Thank you, Oliver, but I am not sure what you want me to do.'

'Nothing Jurgen, nothing at all – for now.'

General Hoeven drew in his rod, gently spooling the line: 'there is one thing that is odd Lancet. Hitler had a long discussion in his office a few weeks ago with Field Marshall Rommel. I know the Field Marshall dislikes the Chancelry. There was a rumour he had drawn up war plans, but it is probably scuttlebutt.'

'You are correct, my old friend, probably scuttlebutt.' Lancet replied

Neither man noticed the glint of binoculars or the slight rustling of grass on the opposite shoreline. Tobias Fox brushed away leaves before slipping away.

There were ructions that very afternoon at the House of Commons. Baldwin was swinging in the wind. Churchill knew the alternatives were miserable. The PM was a weak man. There were cabinet members who were worse. They were either unwitting marionettes of Hitler or execrable dummies.

'Do something Lancet. Do something now. Our country is at stake', Churchill said in a rare telephone call to the Cage.

'I have a plan,' Oliver Lancet replied.

'It may be our final chance, Oliver. My bones tell me that war is looming. Our army is embarrassingly small and our equipment is obsolete. Do something Oliver now. I want to destroy the Huns and unless we wake up from our torpor England will be over. Do something.'

12

SCOTLAND – BERLIN - SCOTLAND

The new season's bottling was always a time of excitement at the distillery. Tobias and his brothers were satisfied with the yield. The Pedro Ximenez casks procured from a broker in Edinburgh proved to be of high quality. The casks originally came from Portugal and were previously filled with delectable sherry. The brothers agreed the blend was among the best produced by the distillery. The salty spray, the peat and the finest barley combined to create a dram that stood with the choicest single malts distilled in Islay. The whisky was supple yet plump and tasted of apple, shortbread and nutmeg. It was a triumph.

Despite the success of the blend Tobias Fox was wracked with sadness. His brothers noticed. They could not help but notice. He accepted the pats on the back and the effusive praise from visiting whisky buyers with wan thanks, but every night he slunk back to his room with a bottle. They could hear the old rages and howls, they remembered from the time he returned from the Irish prison. But there was more. This rage and anguish were different. This was visceral. They left him alone. There was nothing they could do.

'It was the letter from Berlin.' The brothers believed they could trace Tobias's slump into despair to the letter. They were on the money.

It was not that Sarah Wagner wanted corroboration that Tobias Fox was working for British Intelligence. She believed Oliver Lancet. She hated the man, but this did not stop her believing him. There was corroboration though. It came in an unlikely way. On the very next day Sarah delivered a vase of mixed blooms to the British Embassy. She was arranging the flowers on a handsome walnut side cabinet when Bill Masterson walked by. He stopped to chat.

'How are you Mrs Wagner? I trust the shop is doing well. There are a lot of English in town. I have been worked off my feet'.

Sarah Wagner doubted this statement. Masterson was, as usual, bleary eyed and red faced. He was a tippler – that she could tell.

'We have had a succession of London spivs in Berlin drumming up new business. At least I was given a damned fine whisky. Tobias Fox blends a great Speyside dram, despite being one of London's bum boys.'

Sarah was taken aback. She retained her equilibrium.

'Mr Fox visited my café on several occasions. He did not strike me as a homosexual'.

'I am sorry to be so crude. I meant that he is a spook. He works for a fellow called Oliver Lancet. You may not remember him. I brought him to your café'.

'Oh yes', Sarah replied, 'I remember him well'.

She returned to the shop with renewed anger and shame. She realised in bringing an English spy to her home she put them all at risk. 'We are probably under scrutiny', she thought now her son was working virtually next door to the Fuhrer's office.

If she loved Tobias Fox momentarily, she hated him now.

Sarah Wagner penned the missive. She tore it up, made herself a coffee, paced around and wrote the letter again. It was no more placatory than her first version. She posted it anyway.

'Dear Tobias,

I write this letter while angry and feeling foolish. Angry because you are a false man and feeling foolish because I was taken in by your bluff Scottish blarney.

I have met with a snake, a man called Lancet. You probably know of the meeting. I find out you are a snake of the same breed. You disgust me. For a moment you made me feel I had a friend and a lover, now I know you have an agenda. You befriended me for a purpose. Lancet told me he knows of my Jewish father. Though he made no direct threat it was implicit.

I am sad for poor Tom. He loves you. He even sees you as the father he never knew. I have not disabused him. As far as poor Tom is concerned you have left Berlin forever.

Do not contact me again.
Sarah Wagner'

Tobias read and re-read the letter. He poured a mighty dram of double cask strength single malt and drank deeply. He felt the heat of the whisky scald his throat. He sobbed with his head in his hands. He never had a son, but young Tom touched his soul. The lad was so vulnerable. He thought of the day Sarah, Mutte, Tom and Poppy accompanied him to the countryside. They supped on strudel and wine sitting in the town square of a village. They talked as a family. Sarah had never seen Tom so alive and talkative.

Tobias's brothers could hear his moaning. 'The black dog has struck again', the elder brother said. The younger brother agreed.

Tobias fell on his bed and slept fitfully. As he lay, he chanted 'that bastard Lancet, that bastard Lancet, let him rot in hell'.

Tobias woke from his fitful sleep. It was mid-morning. He showered, dressed and strode down to Aggies Caf for a full Scottish breakfast of eggs, sausages, sheep's heart, haggis and thick highland bacon. He washed the meal down with three cups of Tartan Tea. The Glasgow bus was on time, and he boarded carrying a small leather portmanteau. The bus took him to the Central Port. He spoke to the harbour-master's office showing his Secret Service credentials and walked the wharves until he found the Scottish steamer bound for Berlin. He boarded using the credentials and paying cash, borrowed from his brothers, for his passage.

When the ship arrived in Berlin Tobias Fox took a tram to the central city and using a fake passport booked in at a pensione. He made a call.

'General, your spectacles are ready. Do you want me to bring them to the Military College or would you prefer to pick them up at the shop'.

'I will pick them up this afternoon. I suppose you need to check the fit and prescription. Will three this afternoon be suitable'.

'Certainly, General I will see you then'.

General Jurgen Hoeven put the phone down and wondered! It was Lancet's call sign, but he was not expecting him. Still perhaps it was part of the grand plan. He informed his secretary he would be away for an hour in the afternoon and went back to marking exam papers.

13

BERLIN

Doctor Goebbels was fascinated by modern medicine. He was particularly taken by the research of a Dr Josef Mengele. Goebbels had always referred to himself as Doctor Goebbels. His business cards and the gold leaf on his office door was embossed with his title. His doctoral thesis was in literature. Goebbels always had a fascination with medical matters. This probably related to his own lifelong infirmity of a deformed foot. Despite his disability and his own suspect Aryan provenance [his mother was Dutch], Goebbels was fixated with ensuring that mixed and inferior races were weeded out of the new German Aryan super stock. He shared Hitler's preoccupation with this holy grail.

Doctor Mengele was making waves. The young academic had published papers discussing genetic experimentation. He was a follower of Dr Karl Merz, a neurosurgeon who published journal articles elucidating the research into neuro activity being carried out at the Berlin Brain Surgery Academy. Merz was the chief of surgery at the institution. The academy was situated on the outskirts of the city in a purpose built and closely guarded building surrounded by a high chain wire fence patrolled by Wehrmacht troops. The hospital was directly under the auspices of Hitler himself. Grotesque operations were carried out on lemur monkeys, chimpanzees and dogs. So far attempts to transfer brains from one animal to another, whether of same species or not, failed miserably. The shifting of brain lobes, from right to left, in a chimpanzee was claimed to be more successful, but some of the assistants were less convinced of the positivity of the outcome. The chimpanzee from then on refused to obey commands and, the assistants conjectured the monkey bore a deep resentment to be taken from swinging happily on nutmeg trees with his friends to his present situation caged in a research laboratory and prodded, poked and cut open by doctors and scientists. The research became, at least, local news when Dr Merz claimed that he transferred the 'happy' right frontal lobe of a chimpanzee to the 'sad' left posterior lobe. It was true that the chimp was a good deal more unhappy after the operation than before.

'I would be unhappy if some bastard opened my brain and spent hours shifting my lobes around', said a Bavarian research assistant.

'I would be surprised if you would even notice', his pert biologist companion replied, 'all the doctors would be doing is spooning porridge.'.

The international Press Corp in Berlin were amused by the story. A bluff Aussie news hound said to his New Zealand counterpart over lagers, 'in your mob's case, he could try transferring a sheep's brain to a kiwi to see if there is improved perceptive skills'.

The New Zealander was not offended. 'In your case if a kangaroo brain was transplanted, at least you could hop faster and have a shot of beating me to a story'. An English journalist nearby laughed at the banter and the Kiwi turned to him, 'transplanting a pig's brain into a Pommy may clean you buggers up a bit'.

The German Press was positive, though careful. 'Early tests are promising,' and 'an exciting breakthrough may be on the horizon.'

Goebbels and Hitler earnestly discussed the article by Dr Merz.

'It is little use operating on Jews or gipsies', said Hitler, 'their brains are inferior. It would be interesting to find an Aryan with a defect and see if a lobotomy can be curative.'

Goebbels uneasily shifted in his seat. He knew he was far from the perfect specimen of the master race. When he spoke to Hitler, he aways sought to hide his congenital stutter.

Hitler continued to muse:

'Find out what Merz can do to improve our race. There are many flawless Aryans but there are others who are short of perfection. Take a man who is clever, even brilliant but who has a defect that diminishes his worth. This is the area of research that may produce useful results.'

Goebbels wondered if Hitler was thinking of Goring, a brilliant tactician but who drank excessively and wore make up and silk gowns when entertaining; 'or me' he thought 'with my stammer and gammy leg'.

When Dr Merz arrived at the Chancelry he was met by Heinrich Beck, who escorted him to Goebbels office. As they walked the halls Merz studied Beck. He took in the goose-step, the ridiculous haircut and the slack jaw. He decided a lobotomy would make no difference to the fellow as one could not turn a sow's ear into a silk purse.

Minister Goebbels remained seated when Dr Merz arrived.

'It is indeed a pleasure Herr Doctor. The Fuhrer sends his apologies. We are intent on ensuring our young men and women are prime examples of Aryan superiority. Birth defects and intellectual weaknesses are rare, but we want to find if your study of genetics has led you to any conclusions. For example, can you improve physical performance or remove mental blockages.'

'We are well advanced in many areas of eugenics', Merz replied, 'but we have been focusing on the more negative aspects of the science. The sterilisation of Jews and gipsies, euthanasia of the aged, infirm and retarded are the relatively easy goals we have been studying. These steps will improve the race as intermarriage or haphazard sexual consort will inevitably be diminished'.

Merz spoke matter-of-factly. He could have been discussing cough medicine or a cure for shingles. Even Dr Goebbels who enjoyed pulling the wings off insects as a child felt a chill.

'Can you improve the intelligence of a human'.

'Yes, in certain circumstances we can enhance cognition and emotional responses. It depends on the person, but there has been some very encouraging research into the methodology of curing autism. The Austrian physician Hans Asperger has done valuable work in this field. Autistic people have difficulty projecting emotion. They are described as being shut in personalities.'

Goebbels listened carefully. 'Can you improve a person's id? Can they be made more intelligent or more aware? For example, you met my assistant Heinrich Beck. He was waiting for you. He is very eager but lacks subtlety. Can you dial up his intelligence'?

Merz chuckled, 'too stupid', he replied.

14

BERLIN

The park on the Northern edge of Pankow was a dusty unkempt square with a murky lake that even the wood ducks avoided. Sea gulls scavenged on the perimeter and fought for scraps with ravens that sat in the nearby plane trees watching for food left by the office workers who lunched on the rickety benches.

When General Hoeven arrived at the park it was almost deserted. It was a clear day, but if there was wind in the city it seemed inevitably to find its way to Pankow. One seat was occupied by a bulky man who was made bulkier by his thick grey overcoat. He waved to Hoeven who made his way across the dirt and grass. The ravens and gulls watched him closely. They did not see him as a threat, but rather a potential source of food. He carried no bag, but the birds knew that pockets sometimes carried sandwiches and when eaten there would be crumbs and perhaps a shred of liverwurst.

The bulky man was Tobias Fox.

'Good afternoon, General, you do not know me, but I know of you', he said.

'Who are you, how do you possess Oliver Lancet's call sign and what do you want'? Hoeven said.

'My name is Tobias Fox. I work for Oliver Lancet. He does not know I am here. As for his call sign – I am a field agent. My skills are the dark arts of gathering information unlike Lancet who is an exponent of the black arts of subterfuge and deceit.'

'What do want from me'

'I was sent to Berlin earlier this year by Lancet to strike up a friendship with the Wagner boy – the barber. I met his mother and was welcomed into the family. Oliver Lancet has a grand plan. Not that I have been entrusted with it.

Lancet works on a need not to know basis. My cover was exposed by Lancet. I am worried that Lancet will use young Tom Wagner, the barber, to get the information he wants then sacrifice his family. I am going to run the op, whether Lancet likes it or not.'

'So, you are Robert the Bruce, the Scottish hero come to the aid of the family. Why would you be so brave? Do you have a yen for the woman or the barber? You realise the Chancelry is a fortress. What do you intend to do? Storm the ramparts.'

'That is why I am here'.

Tobias summed up the man. He seemed more a scholar than a soldier, with his spectacles and grey hair. He ignored the man's chide. He would simply press on with his inquiry. There would be no explanation or exposition.

'How did you even know my circumstance'? General Hoeven asked.

'I am a spy. I served in Ireland. Oliver Lancet is fine and dandy in an office in Soho, but when he goes fishing in the English countryside, he does not know to look over his shoulder. You are just as bad. You are lucky Goebbels has not already sniffed you out. You have no tradecraft. If Lancet has enlisted your help, you will need a bloody babysitter'.

'Perhaps that is your task.' Hoeven replied.

'No, it is not! Take it up with Lancet. When you were fishing together, I could not hear your conversation, but you said something to Lancet just before you left that made him stand stock-still. We are both parts of his masterplan, but I do like to know how many pieces there are on the board. Can you enlighten me?'

'General Rommel has allegedly, on instructions from Hitler, prepared a War Plan. The Fuehrer is supposed to be most chuffed by its masterful simplicity. Rumour has it he keeps it on his desk and examines it frequently.'

'And that is what you told Lancet?'

'Yes,' General Hoeven replied.

'For some reason Oliver blew my cover. I will let you know what I want from you when I know myself. Do not tell Lancet we met. Do not tell anybody'.

Tobias rose and left the park.

Parrott was sitting sipping coffee in a small café bordering the park. He had been watching Hoeven and Fox through binoculars.

'It seems that the pieces are in place', he said to his companion.

Harry Lime rose and slipped out the rear door.

Tobias Fox after leaving the park doubled back quickly. He had seen the row of shops and identified the café as a perfect perch to watch the meeting. He was not surprised to see Harry Lime emerge. The man had many strings dangling in the air. He was even less surprised to see Parrott getting into the rear of a black limousine.

'Moving the pawns on the board', he said to himself.

Later that evening Parrott caught the mail flight home to London. At an airport on the other side of Berlin Harry Lime boarded a cargo plane bound for Vienna.

Poppy finished work and left the Chancelry to walk to the square lined with shops nearby. The early evening air was crisp and as the sun set Berliners strolled the pathways around the grassy parkland that stood in the centre of the square. She found a seat and lit a cigarette. It was a ritual for Poppy. She enjoyed her working day with Tom Wagner, but the nights were dreary. The food in the hostel was usually bland and the company leaden. Occasionally she would go dancing with Yvette and Marlena, but their conversation was vapid. They were interested in boys, clothes and dancing. It was all they spoke of, and, in any event, they only talked about themselves. Occasionally they would ask about Poppy's work, but they were not really interested. When Tom Wagner first came to the Chancelry, they casually questioned Poppy about him, but they heard he was odd, 'a bit strange', it was said. They lost interest. A mental barber was of no appeal, even for a romp.

She took a drag on her cigarette and contemplated the bustle of the park. Families were walking dogs; little boys were kicking footballs and old geezers were plodding along talking earnestly. There were a few

Nazis in their black shirts, marching about harassing people. They left Poppy alone. Some would have been aware she worked at the Chancelry.

She noticed a man walking in her direction. He was wearing a deer stalker hat that almost covered his ears but the walk, she remembered the walk. It was the rolling gait of a man used to climbing hills and traversing valleys. It was Tobias Fox. She met the man with Tom Wagner and his family. He ate at their home, and once she joined him and his family for a Sunday drive. She remembered enjoying chilled white wine at a town square. She even wondered if Tom's mother hankered for the fellow. They seemed so easy and comfortable together, but recently she had not heard his name mentioned by the family. Poppy was not an inquisitive young woman. She liked her privacy and respected the privacy of others. However, she recalled, awhile ago, his name came up somehow and she asked Sarah a question.

'Has Tobias gone back home'?

It was greeted with silence and a long look from Frau Wagner to Mutte. The look said, 'say nothing'. Poppy took the hint and put her enquiry away, but the man was now walking towards her. His walk was resolute and his gaze intent. Poppy, somehow, understood she was his goal.

He sat on the bench next to Poppy.

'How are the Wagner family? Is Tom happy'? he asked.

'I thought you went back to Scotland. Your name is never mentioned. The family seemed sad when I once spoke of you. I wondered if you let them down. Tom does not talk about you, but his malady prevents him remembering the past. He lives in the present'.

'I know', Tobias Fox replied, 'he only lives in black and white, like a film. That is why you are so important to him. I do not know your back story. My guess you have much to hide and you hide it well'.

'Are you threatening me Herr Fox, if so, it will not work. I have lived my life surrounded by bullies. They do not frighten me'.

Tobias Fox threw up his arms. 'No Poppy, I am no bully. I am here to enlist your aid. I want to keep the Wagner family safe. I believe they are at risk on two fronts.'

'At risk, what do you mean Sarah Wagner is a florist. Her son cuts hair'.

'I have reason to believe that British Intelligence – spions – are seeking help from the Wagner family. I believe they have made threats to Sarah. Any help the family give will be accompanied by great danger. Young Tom is vulnerable.'

'They should go to the authorities. Tom could make a complaint. There is an arsehole called Heinrich Beck who spends half his day hanging round our salon. I am not sure if he fancies me or Tom. He works for Goebbels. Spying is what Huns are good at. We could give Beck something to do.'

'The Wagner family has Jewish roots Poppy'.

Poppy remained silent. She knew what this meant.

'I work for a man named Oliver Lancet. He is a senior officer in British Intelligence. He saved me from an Irish prison, though my guess is he put me there in the first place. He is using the Wagner family and me. I am not sure of the mechanics of his plan, but I do know it is dangerous. I can look after myself.

The Wagner family have no such ability. I do not like being a pawn in the game of Oliver Lancet.'

'This is terrible Mr Fox, but it has nothing to do with me. I am a hairdresser's assistant. I like Tom but I am merely an acquaintance of the Wagner family'.

'I may need your help. You say you are a mere acquaintance, but I believe you have feelings for Tom. I have seen you together, but that is only half the equation. Hitler is crazy as a loon. He will set the world on fire. I believe you hate the Nazis as much as I do. If I am wrong go back to the Chancelry and tell Heinrich Beck. I will be arrested and shot. Otherwise, the next time you see me I will be in German Army uniform. Greet me pleasantly as if you know me, that is all I ask. It will help save Tom and his mother.'

Tobias Fox rose and walked away without looking back. Poppy watched him leave the park and disappear in one of the cobbled narrow laneways leading to the nearby highway. She pondered. Then she left the park and puffing on a cigarette made her way back to the Chancelry.

She was greeted, at the gate, by the two young guards.

'Have you had a pleasant stroll, Poppy', one asked.

'Very pleasant', she replied, 'Berlin is beautiful this time of the year'.

'No young fellows seeking your attention', said the other cheeky guard.

'I did not notice, but how could I with two such handsome hunks like you two waiting for me', with that she doffed an imaginary hat leaving the two young guards laughing.

15

BERLIN

'Oliver Lancet was sitting drinking hot chocolate at the usual meeting place when he laid down the law to Sarah.

'There is a document Mrs Wagner, required by Churchill, that Hitler keeps in his office. We are still sorting out a plan of action, but as your son works next door, we will need his co-operation. We are conscious of his disability, but his very proximity carries risk. It is time, perhaps, to gently tell him that life is not all shaving suds and cologne.'

Sarah Wagner wondered what to do. 'Should she sit her son down and bluntly inform him of the cold hard facts? How would he react? Could he be trusted to remain silent? His disability often caused him to simply blurt out whatever had happened. Hitler would be likely to take a dim view of his barber purloining state secrets so his mother could hand them over to a foreign power, particularly England.'

She was reluctant to tell Mutte of her problem. Her mother-in-law was never told her son was marrying a Jew. There was always a touch of prejudice in Germany. The toffs, the old Prussian family scions, treated Jews as lesser beings. Her late father-in-law came from just such a family. Many Jews were successful business owners, doctors, advocates and engineers. It was said the Kaiser had Jewish blood. But it was not enough – these days prejudice was ugly and rampant. Jews were leaving the city in droves. Shiploads of Jewish children were rumoured to be gone, ferried to the new world. The new black and brown shirts with their slack jaws and stupid hair cuts marched around Berlin smashing the windows of Jewish shops and chanting inane slogans. 'Toten Juden' they shouted as they swaggered down streets splitting strolling families and knocking over the odd elderly man or woman who failed to get out of their way quickly enough.

'These stupid boys are nothing but future cannon fodder for Hitler and his maniacs', Mutte would say to her daughter-in-law. 'They are mainly uneducated fools who are envious of success. The Jews work hard and care for their families. Their liverwurst is much better than the crude sausages that we must buy these days'.

Sarah felt she was ready to tell her mother-in-law of her family antecedents. Sarah's parents did not attend the wedding. It was a hurried affair as the baby bump was showing. Sarah left an unhappy home. Her mother was a daily drinker and un unfaithful wife. Her father was a bitter man. He believed he was denied his proper place in Saville Row because of his wife. He took out his unhappiness on his daughter. He saw her as the spawn that held him back. The best tailor in Whitechapel was a booby prize.

'We have never discussed it Mutte, but my father was Jewish'.

'I know that silly girl. Your Pa was a bloody tailor in Whitechapel, of course he was a kike. My father was a cobbler in Munich, but I had a pretty face, shapely legs and a good pair of titties. I scored an officer. Do you think I did not check your story before the marriage. Up the duff or not if you came from Romany or Eskimo stock you would not have married my son, but Juden – so what! You did the right thing in getting out of Whitechapel. You saved yourself from a miserable life in London, made my son happy and brought young Tom into the world, bless him'.

The two women hugged. Tom walked in and they broke apart laughing. He was fiddling his hands and swaying.

'Is everything all right Ma,' he asked.

'Never better,' Sarah answered, but she was churning inside. She knew storm clouds were forming.

When Tom ambled away to clean his equipment Sarah told Mutte of her predicament. Mutte murmured imprecations. She damned Tobias to hell. The two women sat in the front room at the rear of the house and over a bottle of white wine discussed their plight. Mutte won the day. She was adamant.

'Hitler is a lunatic, a lunatic with bad hair, even young Tom cannot shape it. He will lead the German people into another war. I know nothing much about history, but I cannot understand how a whole country can be sucked in by the Nazi bullshit. It is one thing for the cretinous youth in their black shirts and tight shorts to march around spouting their stupid slogans.

They are jealous of the success of others. They resent the Jews because they work hard and save their marks. I can even understand the haus frau, the wives whose reading stops at cookbooks and who spend their days chattering in cafes spreading gossip. I cannot work out how the rest, the workers – men and women have fallen in line. Do we come from a breed of Bavarian sheep'.

Mutte paused and swigged a healthy gulp of the sweet wine.

'There is no need to tell Tom about your meeting with the English demon. Do not worry him yet. For all we know nothing may happen. We will face each challenge when it turns up.'

Meanwhile Tobias Fox was deep in reflection. He was pondering as to how he could reconcile with the Wagner family. He gave thought to inventing a legend, a false explanation. He decided against it. He was sick of lying and sick of Oliver Lancet.

16

LONDON - BERLIN

Winston Churchill was in Pall Mall. He was making one of his rare visits to central London. He dined at the Garrick Club with three of his supporters.

'That fool Baldwin still believes Hitler has no ambition to invade England. He thinks he is only interested in recovering the German speaking lands in Eastern Europe, parts of Poland and Rumania. Our PM is an idiot. He misunderstands the German people. They are still smarting for losing the Great War. Every man and woman felt the loss of a husband, wife, cousin, friend or neighbour. The hospitals still house burn victims who will be there for life. They are a proud people'.

An old friend, a correspondent for the Times of London was one of the guests:

'Surely, they are tired of war, Winston. There comes a time when the women will tell the men to stop, tell them to work the crops and feed the animals.'

Winston lit another cigar. It was his third Monte Cristo for the day. He blew gusts of smoke into the air. It settled on the next table where a group of Law Lords were discussing easements and torts. They turned

towards Churchill's table but said nothing. They knew
he may be Prime Minister one day.

'Hitler has mesmerised the German people with
his oratory. Do not forget Berlin is a hub of great
learning. Scientists, engineers and philosophers thrive.
Many of the great thinkers are Jewish. Most of the
engineers and manufacturers are Jewish', he paused
and blew another gust, this time purposely in the
direction of the Law Lords.

'Yet, one man's passionate oratory has turned
the collective brains of the public into apple sauce.
Hundreds of thousands attend his rallies and shout and
curse the Jews. I have heard that worse things are going
on. Supposedly there are obscene medical experiments
being carried out. The practice is called Eugenics.
Doctors are opening brains and trying to shift the lobes
around and adjust the wiring. It is grotesque. About
the only horror they are not yet researching is trying to
turn men into women and vice versa'.

'That would be ridiculous Winston', said an
angular local member from Wales, 'the sexes have
different bodily structures.'

'That won't stop them', Churchill replied, 'the
medical profession is no less odious than the lawyers.
Shakespeare wrote 'kill all the lawyers', he should have
added 'and the doctors as well'. That fool Baldwin
will lead us into a war that we cannot win. We must
immediately re-arm'.

'But Hitler claims he has no interest in the West. He
says he just wants to reconstitute Germany as it was under
the Prussian Kings. If you are to persuade the Commons,
you will need evidence to persuade the Cabinet'.

'I am well aware of that', Churchill replied before sending another gust of tobacco smoke towards the Law Lords. They rose and gathered their bags before leaving the club. Winston watched. He wondered if the retreat of the crusty judges was a good omen.

He left the club shortly afterwards and entered his limousine. Before the vehicle left the curb there was a rap on the door. Oliver Lancet got into the car.

'There are German troop movements on the Polish border. Hitler is not trying to hide it. He says the army is simply performing exercises.'

'I am unsurprised,' Churchill answered. 'I will say it again Lancet. Do something. Get me proof. Give me the means to persuade the soft cocks in the Commons.'

Oliver Lancet alighted the vehicle and returned to the Cage. He knew he would have to act.

The Chancelry in Berlin was alive with activity. The barber's salon was so busy there was a waiting list of officers and bureaucrats. The talk was of military installations, new weapons and army deployment. Tom Wagner seemed oblivious. He would fit a new gown on each customer. He carefully scrubbed each neck with a warm damp cloth; he discussed the cut he would give and begin his work. He swung the gleaming steel scissors with the dexterity of a swordfighter and gently ran the comb and brushes across the scalp. Even the women began seeking his services. Eva Braun, Hitler's mistress, once came for a cut. She was rarely in Berlin, preferring The Eyrie Hitler's mountain hideaway.

'Good riddance' Poppy commented when Eva Braun left the salon.

Eva Braun carried with her an air of arrogant self-importance and a bubbling cauldron of bitterness that lay just below the surface and threatened at any moment to cause her to burst into anger.

'Cut the bitch and Tom was likely to be up before a firing squad', Poppy said to Larry Cromarty and Ronnie Tolar while drinking absinthe one night at the Lady Windermere. The little downstairs dive had opened a new world to Poppy.

She went to the club with the Wagner family one evening. Harry Lime was there. She did not speak to him. He was at the other end of the table. She stole a glance at Harry Lime from time to time. He carried with him an air of ambiguity. It was like a shroud. The dark suit and homburg hat helped. The black bushy eyebrows and the darting tiny eyes added to the mystique. He said little and spoke in a surprisingly soft voice. Poppy only understood a snippet or two of what he said, even when she strained. Larry and Ronnie were different, so different Poppy wondered what drew them to Harry Lime.

'All expatriates' she decided. 'All displaced from home'.

But Larry and Ronnie were so dissimilar to the burly man at the head of the table. They gossiped endlessly about other expatriates, particularly their sexual proclivities and money troubles. There was the Kansas poet caught mounting a monk in the annexe of a Greek Orthodox cathedral and the Welch soprano who 'played for the opposition', Tom Wagner was sitting next to when this latter remark was made, and she had to explain its meaning. He seemed surprised at such goings on.

A constant at the other end of the Bar was Heinrich Beck. He was always alone. He drank silently rarely conversing with his neighbours at the Bar. Poppy ignored him but wondered why he was spending his time at such a raffish hole in the wall. 'Was he spying on the group, perhaps on Tom or was he a secret lech'?

17

BERLIN

Though Goebbels was the Communications Minister in Hitler's Cabinet, it was more a cover for his real work. The communications, such as they were, consisted of feeding the International Press corps with titbits of, mainly false, information. He employed a gaggle of wholesome young women to release press handouts. Goebbels made sure they were well written with catchy headlines. This made it easier for the lazy reporters and sub-editors to print whole slabs of false information without the necessity of doing any work. Consequently, Hitler's lies and exaggerations were often spread without being forensically tested.

Goebbels was also engaged in the introduction of Eugenics to Germany. Hitler craved for an army of young men and women of the finest Aryan stock. Their tall, muscular build, handsome, blue-eyed visages framed by glistening blonde hair would march, as victors, through the cities of the world. At their head would be a train of limousines headed by a white Daimler-Benz in which Hitler would be standing and saluting the adoring crowds of victors and vanquished. Goebbels was not so sure. Many townsfolk were pimply, overweight young men and women. Jam strudels and beef stews were stodgy and loaded with fat. The rural young people were healthier, but their fitness seemed to be at odds with their intelligence. Goebbels hoped Hitler did not under-estimate the task ahead.

Dr Karl Merz was waiting for Goebbels at the clinic. The gate was manned by two guards of the newly formed Waffen SS troop of special force soldiers. Himmler, another of Hitler's coterie, established the corps. It was to contain only native Germans of Aryan stock. Goebbels examined the guards. They fitted the bill.

'We have looked forward to this meeting', said Dr Merz, 'I have been liaising with my confreres Dr Mengele and Dr Asperger. We have discussed various ways that the Aryan race may be improved by simple brain surgery. We have had some success with monkeys, but the operations carried out on Gipsies and criminals have not brought much solace. We have, so far, kept the press away, but we have a large staff, and they are only human. People talk'.

Goebbels accompanied the doctor and a retinue of assorted staff along the seemingly endless hallways. Chattering noises could be heard as they entered a room where a dozen cages containing rhesus monkeys stood on a long bench. When the group entered the noise increased and the monkeys, as if knowing their intended fate, began screaming and banging on their cages.

'They are slightly noisier than the Gipsies', said Dr Merz, 'and even less intelligent'.

Goebbels was glad to leave the room which smelt of damp fur and monkey scat. They passed through a chainmail gate into a row of cells.

'Our patients' said the doctor.

Each cell contained a young adult. There were burly bearded jews, swarthy Mediterranean types and slick dark gypsies. Most were men, but there was a gypsy woman with flaming red hair and a broken nose. She let loose as they passed.

'You fugging dirty Nazis, I bet most of you have little pudding basters. You probably prefer it up your backsides'. Her eyes fastened on Goebbels, 'and you, you little gremlin, you look like Goebbels. Have you a club foot and a tiny pestle'?

'An Irish gypsy', said Dr Merz, 'to turn her into a lady will stretch the limits of the science'.

Later they settled into a handsome lounge, drank execrable coffee and ate cake.

Dr Merz made his pitch. 'We are ready to start our real work. A lobotomy can settle an Irish biddy or silence a Rhesus monkey, but the new theory of Eugenics will enable us to cure personality disorders and improve brain power. Imagine an army of Aryan Gods who can not only outrun but out-think an enemy. Germans will rule the world'.

Goebbels returned to his office with his retinue.

'Beck', he said to Heinrich, 'I want you to prepare a report. Use a dictionary. Your spelling errors are tiresome. We will then form a work party to identify possible candidates for brain surgery. We should find a young person with unfulfilled potential. Perhaps he has a lisp or a facial tic. Perhaps he possesses an unfortunate personality trait. Prepare the report and I will take it to the Fuehrer'.

18

LONDON - BERLIJN

Churchill called a press conference. Journalists trooped down to Chartwell in buses. The BBC was there in force. A small army of technicians set up microphones, connected to a generator carried in a van. Producers fussed around and a news radio anchor strutted around pompously performing ugly lip exercises to ensure his baritone was at its most mellifluous.

Churchill's household staff watched. They gave each other knowing looks when an engineer was berated by a poncy producer or there was argument about the pitch of the bass sound. The rest of the pack were a mixed bag. The penny dreadful gossip rags were represented by ill dressed, spotty young men in cheap suits. The great daily journalists were in elegant flannels. There were many photographers. A gaggle of assorted public servants were on hand to help. Baldwin sent three grey ghosts to record the proceedings. 'Was Churchill about to mount a challenge' or 'was he just making a gouty set of complaints and boasts.'

Oliver Lancet stood quietly at the rear of the crowd. He was hoping the old man would not make any outlandish promises or blurt out information of their conversations. Not that Lancet ever gave much away, but Churchill had a bee in his bonnet about his mole. General Hoeven would be valuable one day, but Lancet was hoping he was not going to be sacrificed for a retarded barber.

Winston Churchill emerged from the mansion. He was accompanied by his current private secretary. They did not last long. They were either fired in a rage or left ashen and shaking. He faced the crowd with the rising sun behind him. The journalists squinted and placed files over their foreheads to obtain a clearer view. Churchill surveyed the scene with satisfaction.

'Baldwin is no Prime Minister', he commenced, 'a wild beast cannot be satiated. All the Prime Minister seeks to ensure is that we will be the last country to be over-run. Bullies only have one master and that is brute force. I love my country and have risked my life many times to preserve our freedoms and customs. As our fellow citizens wend their way back to England from the continent they are sharing their observations. Jews are being murdered and the sick killed in the name of medicine. Even our beloved European Pikeys are sent to camps and tortured'.

Oliver Lancet smiled wryly. 'Pikey was a slang word for Romany or Gipsy. It was the first time he had heard Churchill even use the word. 'Our Winston enjoyed demonstrating he had the common touch,'

The old statesman finished his speech with a rousing shout out to King and Country. There was a hubbub of, sometimes insolent probing from the reporters which Churchill batted away easily. He took a question from a BBC grandee.

'Are you planning to challenge the PM'.

'Definitely not', Churchill replied, 'if change takes place, it will be organic'.

'What do you know of Hitler's war machine. Does he even have the troops and guns to invade France, let alone England'.

The speaker was a pompous Frenchman. He was a senior correspondent with a Cambridge degree and an ego to match. He spoke in the strange patois of an Oxbridge graduate blended with 5th Arondissement Parisian. Churchill looked him over with undisguised contempt.

'You better hope we are ready. All invading armies of your country ever see is a flotilla of fleeing backsides'.

There was some repressed mirth amongst the rabble. The questions petered out and Churchill turned on his heel and left. Oliver Lancet breathed a sigh of relief and hailed his driver.

Hitler, Goring, Himmler and Goebbels listened to the broadcast in the Fuehrer's state room.

'Will he seize control'? asked Himmler.

'I doubt it', Goebbels replied, 'the man is a drunkard'.

Goring was bullish. 'Our air force can blow their little island into the middle of the Atlantic Ocean.'

"I would not be too sure', said Himmler, 'we must continue to ready ourselves'.

Hitler took it all in. He believed in his own destiny. One day he would rule the world.

Ronnie Tolar, the loose young expatriate chanteuse, sat on the bed of the apartment she shared with Larry Cromarty listening to the broadcast. Both were drawing on Turkish cigarettes.

'Should we leave'? she asked.

'Where and how', Larry replied, 'we have no money and now Harry Lime has gone back to Vienna we have nobody to borrow from'.

'Harry Lime predicted a war. He told me to hitch my wagon to that fellow Tobias Fox. He will get you out of Dodge, he said, whatever that means?'

'It is an American allusion to the new Cowboy movie films. Is the Scotchman even here? I have not seen him at the Lady Windermere'.

'We will haunt the place until we see him', said Ronnie.

'We always haunt the place', Larry replied.

'Harry Lime also said something odd'. she said. 'He told me we will have to pay our way, 'it won't be money', he said. 'Your ingenuity will be tested. You are a brave young woman. That is why you will be called on'. What the hell did he mean?'

'Did he mention me?' asked Larry Cromarty, ignoring the question. Ronnie often posed questions to which there was no answer required.

'Your name did not come up', she replied.

Tobias Fox also listened to the broadcast in his pensione. Time was on the wing. He was needed in Speyside. His brothers were desperate. The barley was ready to juice. He poured himself a dram. 'The cards are beginning to fall,' he murmured to himself.

19

BERLIN

Joseph Goebbells ignored the constant talk of war in the Chancelry. He was obsessed by his study of Eugenics. He was determined the German race would be pure. The young man Heinrich Beck had given him information that piqued his interest. It seemed there may be a person ripe for eugenic operative treatment working in the Chancelry. If Goebbels had believed in a God, the subject would have been Heaven-sent. The likely prospect was tall, handsome and spoke in a deep manly voice. The fellow's dead father was a fallen German hero. Though the mother was English she was a handsome woman, well built, with a fine complexion and clear eyes.

Goebbels went to find the subject. When he entered the salon, the barber was shaving an elderly Oberst from Ordinance. The man almost leapt from the chair in a show of deference causing Tom Wagner to pull his blade back sharply, thereby avoiding cutting the Oberst's throat.

'Be careful Oberst', Goebbels said, 'we want to save you for the battlefield'.

The Oberst nevertheless had left the chair and was standing to attention. He was a strange sight as Tom had only completed half of the shave and none of the haircut. On one side of his face lather dripped down his chin. Poppy handed him a towel, and he gratefully wiped himself before hurriedly escaping.

'I hope I am not so frightening that you would cut my nose off', Goebbels said to Tom who was wiping down his razor, seemingly unperturbed by losing a client in such odd circumstances.

Tom examined Goebbels. 'Your nose is safe, though you have some tufts of hair growing in each nostril that should be removed. I have special clippers for this purpose.'

Goebbels looked carefully at the man and involuntarily felt his nostrils. He inspected Tom. 'Was the man insulting him? There were hairs. Or perhaps was young Heinrich Beck onto something'.

'Are you satisfied with your conditions of service Wagner? Do you want to be a barber for the rest of your life?'

Tom Wagner weighed Goebbels' question carefully. The man seemed serious. But what could he mean? What job would please me more than carefully shaping hair? He finally responded.

'I would enjoy being a bus driver. The sights of Berlin are very interesting, and I could learn the stops', he paused, 'but they are all well marked by signage. I do not think I would miss them. I would make the signs larger, perhaps make the print a greater contrast'.

Poppy intervened. She was not frightened of Dr Goebbels, despite his reputation. The barber's salon was in the Fuehrer's private office suite. More importantly they had a full book.

'Doctor Goebbels, we have customers waiting. One is a General. We are very busy. If you wish to talk with Herr Wagner I can make a suitable time.'

She opened the door to reveal two officers sitting in the waiting area. Poppy was not sure why Goebbels was watching Tom with the leer of a cat about to sup on a juicy trout. It made her uncomfortable. She realised that she took a risk being so disrespectful. She sought to temper her remarks.

'I am sorry Minister, but we have a very busy schedule.'

Goebbels saw the two waiting officers were watching the conversation. One was a Waffen SS General. The Minister nodded to them and left.

Goebbels was satisfied that the young barber should be examined by Dr Merz. There was something odd about the fellow that deserved further scrutiny. As he left the Salon he poked his fingers into his nostrils. 'Yes, there was hair there. The man was correct.'

The two officers in the waiting area observed Goebbels leave. When he poked his fingers in his nostrils, they looked at one another. The General lifted an eyebrow.

While Goebbels was interrogating Tom Wagner and worrying Poppy, Tobias Fox was on the move. It was becoming clear to him that Hitler was close to lighting up Europe. He expected the remaining Jews in Germany would be rounded up. There were reports of death camps and execution squads. He owed nothing to Oliver Lancet. The man was using him. He expected Lancet's view was that an over-the-hill Scotsman was a small price to pay for even a gibbet of information.

After a hearty German breakfast Tobias walked it off. He set off at a brisk pace and by late morning he was standing outside the building where Ronnie Tolar and Larry Cromarty lived. It was a down-at-heel rooming house. The 'No Vacancy' sign looked as if it had not been shifted in years. There was a spider's web that almost covered the sign and was attached to the beech tree that stood sentinel in the front yard. There were six door buzzer buttons. The Ronnie Tolar bell was framed in a hand painted heart. He pressed the bell and almost immediately there was the sound of scampering feet and creaking boards as stairs were descended. The door was opened by Ronnie. She swung it wildly and appeared in the doorway as an actress might enter centre stage.

'Oh, it is not him', she exclaimed.

'Well, it is me but not the 'him' that you were expecting. Remember me. I first met you at The Lady Windermere'.

Ronnie Tolar seemed uncertain. 'The Lady Windermere, oh yes, we danced and drank Cointreau. I remember'.

'No, you don't recall. I am a Jock. You were sitting at Harry Lime's table. I was a friend of Sarah Wagner. You and I neither danced nor drank Cointreau.'

Ronnie had not let him in. She was still standing in the doorway.

'I remember you now. Larry asked after you the other day, but somebody said your name was mud. You must have spurned Sarah Wagner. She is my friend I do not see how I can let you in'?

There were more sounds of floorboards creaking and Larry Cromarty appeared. He was clad in a purple velvet bath robe, and his hair was in curlers.

'Let him in Ronnie. He is a whisky distiller. If he has broken just one heart, he has a long way to go before he catches up with you. The German wolf who you are expecting lives permanently with the knowledge that you flirt shamelessly with any man you meet. He exists with the constancy of a broken heart'.

'My German probably is not coming. I left him last evening for a Yank sailor boy, but he was sick in a taxi, and I came home alone. Fortunately, his perk missed me. The driver was furious, so I jumped out at the first opportunity and high-tailed it'.

Cromarty clapped his hands. He seemed to enjoy Ronnie's sordid little story.

'I am glad you lost the Hun, Ronnie. You see Mr Tobias Fox, it is Tobias isn't it, when Ronnie brings a man home, I must temporarily vacate the room. Sleeping on the old couch in the lobby is an ugly fate. Her German wolf sometimes hires a hotel room. That is more convenient. It means my sleep is not interrupted and Ronnie has shampoo and soap to steal. Even the toilet roll is not safe. She brings it home in her bag.'

Ronnie seemed to have mellowed her view towards Tobias, and she turned on her heel and set off up the stairs. Larry shrugged his shoulders and the two men followed.

Ronnie and Larry shared a room on the second floor. As the three reached the first-floor balcony they passed an open door into an apartment.

'The Goldmans', said Ronnie, 'our friends: He was a Professor of Mathematics, but the Nazis have forced him out of his chair.'

A piano could be heard from within the apartment. 'Frau Goldman', said Ronnie.

They reached the second floor. The pair lived in a large bed-sitting room. There were two single beds, jammed together, at one end of the room and framed in the large bay window was a cane table laden with unwashed plates, glasses and two empty bottles of wine. Neither Ronnie nor Larry made any attempt to clear the mess. Larry gestured to Tobias Fox to sit in an old grey velvet armchair with stuffing coming out of the cushion. Tobias was unworried by the mess. The whisky haulers back home lived in hay lofts and only bathed when they could smell their own odour.

'Is this your only room'? he said, uncharitably.

'We share, with the other guests, a bathroom on the first floor and a kitchen on the ground floor. Not that we cook. Berlin is laden with restaurants. There is no need for us to cook. Ronnie has never boiled an egg, nor laid one though it is not for want of trying'.

Ronnie was squatting on the floor smoking,

'I have many wealthy suitors. They feed us. They know Larry is a bum boy, so they are never jealous. Sometimes I am cast aside for Larry. A lot of these Teutons play on both sides of the street. Not you Mr Fox, you are a Scotty of the old breed. I bet you hunt and fish and drink by a peat hearth with other Scotties.'

'Very poetic', interposed Larry, 'but what can we do for you, Tobias Fox'.

'I am a friend of Mrs Wagner, or more accurately I was a friend of hers. She has gained the impression I am a British spy who was seeking to ingratiate myself with her because her son is a barber in the Chancelry.

I doubt if the Nazi leaders are passing secret plans to one another while getting a shave or haircut. I am concerned for her well-being. These are dangerous times. My disquiet extends to you', Tobias gestured to the pair. 'If the Scheibe hits the fan, only those with money and contacts will get out.'

'Why are you here?' Ronnie asked.

'Mrs Wagner was a friend of mine. I only knew the family for a short time, but I became very fond of them'.

'Sarah particularly', said Ronnie.

'Yes, Sarah particularly; she is a very fine woman, but I am also concerned for the boy. He is an innocent. It is one thing for the Nazis to tolerate him now but if war is declared it will be a different matter. The family could be interned or worse'.

'At least they are not Jewish', said Larry. Tobias did not comment.

Ronnie Tolar rose and rummaged amongst the open bottles on the table. She found what she was looking for. It was a bottle of German cut-price whisky. She took a healthy swig and walked over to Tobias. She seemed angry and was waving the bottle around in an alarming way.

'What the hell are you doing here Tobias Fox? You hardly know us. You are no whisky peddler. You are a bloody spy. Sarah Wagner and I are old friends. She warned me about you. She said do not trust the bastard he is a British secret agent, and they are the worst pricks of all. What do you want from us?'

She took another swig and stood back, swaying a little.

Larry nervously watched his friend.

'Settle down Ronnie, the fellow is our guest. He has come here for a reason'.

'What reason?' She looked accusingly at Tobias Fox. He remained silent and motionless. It was as if he expected the rush of anger.

'What reason? I ask you again. Why, are you here? What do you want from us?' Ronnie Tolar was still weaving around the room, but she was now wheedling not shouting. Her voice tailed off and she crumpled to the floor still clutching the bottle.

'I admit I have ties with British Intelligence. This is Berlin. Every second expat is undercover, either a sleeper or a covert operative. What do you expect? Hitler has designs on world domination. It is no secret. He admits it. The Germans have been mesmerised by the fellow. The world is watching'.

Larry Cromarty was listening carefully.

'Assuming we believe you what has this got to do with us. I am here to gorge myself on young German men and Ronnie is a night club singer carelessly looking for a rich husband'.

'Carelessly?' Ronnie asked.

'That fellow Manfred owns a steel factory, and you will not even open the door, let alone your legs, for him. He calls daily Tobias, and Ronnie either refuses to let him in or opens the window and tells him to bugger off. You called him a smelly Bosch, Ronnie'.

Tobias intervened. It seemed Larry, when in full flight, was loquacious and haphazard to a fault.

'I suppose you would not believe me if I told you I was worried you may be stuck in Berlin when the War breaks out. And it will, if night follows day'.

'What do you want from us?' Ronnie Tolar had settled down. She and Larry Cromarty now watched Tobias Fox intently.

'I have been asked to perform a task for British Intelligence. They believe I owe them. I was in jail in Belfast, and they somehow extricated me. I think they may have put me there, but that is by the by. I have been told that. England needs me. I could not give a fig for England, but I care for Scotland. I do not want Speyside to be overrun by Krauts.'

'But us?' Larry asked.

'Fair question', said Tobias, 'you are acquainted with Harry Lime. I have visited the Lady Windermere. He is presently not to be found. I wish to see him,'

'We have no address or phone number. If Harry Lime wants to be found he will, soon enough, appear'.

'Let him know I want to see him. I may need his help. I expect the British will pay. You may also be useful. This may enable you to get out before Hitler decides to exterminate homos and torch singers.'

Tobias Fox collected himself and left. As he closed the door he turned back to face Ronnie and Larry.

'Watch out for a fellow named Heinrich Beck. He has been hanging round the Lady Windermere. He works for Goebbels. I must go home. I must distil my whisky, but rest assured I will be back.'

20

BERLIN - LONDON

The Berlin Brain Surgery Academy executive staff met to discuss finances. Dr Karl Merz was not only chief surgeon but was the beating heart of the Academy's continual quest for largesse both from the government and business community. The Army was pushing for a battalion of super soldiers. Dr Merz knew he was expected to, somehow, churn out these Aryan Gods. On the other hand, factory owners wanted workers who were compliant, hard working and honest. He realised he had not underplayed his work. The money kept rolling in as Merz and his team experimented with monkey brains. When the trials failed, the animals were cremated. The laboratory left no evidence of the deranged and defaced creatures. The pressure was building on Dr Merz. It was one thing to practise on primates or perform lobotomies on morons. It would be vaguely possible to provide factories manned by idiots to perform simple tasks. Dr Merz was aware the scientists and engineers were working with robotics. Idiots may have a short shelf life. His early work in the science of eugenics did not end well. His efforts in re-assembling human genes led to deaths and deformities. He was able, with some deft politicking, to shift blame and change course. He replaced genetic experimentation with brain lobe re-arrangement. He knew and fretted that one day he would have to produce a viable outcome.

Minister Goebbels was not to be trifled with. He wanted results.

The accountants in the Chancelry were unhappy. The Academy was costing the government money that could be spent on guns, planes and bombs. The doctors and researchers were frustrated. Monkeys and rats were unpleasant patients.

'We will start with gipsies. They have no provenance. There are jew lovers in America and France. I will have some gipsies shipped in'. Dr Merz hoped this would quieten down the naysayers.

In the meantime, Dr Goebbels finally had his haircut by Tom Wagner. During the time he was in the chair he watched the barber closely. He noticed the meticulous way he lined up his scissors and brushes and the orderliness of his work. He compared this with the young man's awkward manner and seemingly random speech.

'Did the magpie come today', Tom asked Poppy during the cut.

'Yes', she replied. 'it was on the ledge earlier'.

'My Mutte makes me apple strudel sometimes', he volunteered, out of the blue.

Poppy was used to Tom's seemingly random remarks and was able to converse happily with him.

'Have you had chocolate strudel', she asked.

'My driver has wide shoulders. Though it may be the tailoring of his coat', Tom replied.

When Goebbels returned to his office he sent for Heinrich Beck,

'You may be correct about the barber. Find out what you can about him. He just cut my hair. He was most competent but made little sense,'

Heinrich Beck left Goebbels office well satisfied. It would be his time to shine. He knew Viktor Wagner, the barber's father, was a genuine war hero. He gave his life for Germany. He was an ace pilot with many kills to show for his bravery but was cut down in his prime. Heinrich Beck was a stupid young man but not stupid enough to attempt to sully the reputation of a war hero. The widow was a different proposition. She was an Englander, an interloper, her antecedents could be searched. If there was a dark secret it could be exposed.

Beck spent time in the central library and the Hall of Records but searching files or scrutinising volumes were tasks that were beyond him. Beck had little to go on. While searching the records he found the article in the German newspaper identifying Sarah Wagner as Sarah Green. The press report about the wedding was prepared before the Jewishness of a person was of significance. He consulted military intelligence in Berlin and found Greenbaum and Rosenberg tailors in the records. A Sarah Greenbaum was identified as a daughter. The officer who gave him the information did not remark on her religion, however the name denoted Jewishness.

He reconnoitred the flower shop, but he learned nothing. Sarah seemed to have a regular and loyal following of nazis, jews and an assortment of customers from the nearby embassies and consulates. He patronised the shop, drank coffee and ate strudel. The pastry was excellent. Beck disliked the taste of coffee and associated the drink with the middle class educated Germans who he perceived looked down on him. Worse still were the coffee-drinking Jewish intellectuals who he despised as being inferior human beings. He stopped coming to the shop when Mrs Wagner began acknowledging him. 'The usual order sir, I have a spiced apple strudel today' or 'I have not seen you for a while, I trust you have been in good health'. He was disconcerted by her pleasantries and could only mutter unintelligible replies. In her turn Sarah Wagner found the new customer odd, but was pleased an obvious nazi, the haircut gave him away, was a customer. She even mentioned him to Mutte.

'A young Nazi is taking his morning break in the café. It is nice to see he appreciates coffee.'

Mutte was unimpressed. 'His preferred beverage would still be bear's piss.'

When a trip to London was broached by Goebbels Heinrich Beck jumped at the chance.

'I hear you are learning English and have gained certification. I will give you an opportunity to put your skills to the test.'

Heinrich Beck had found English lessons in the Chancelry difficult to the point of agony. The teacher was a forbidding Dutch woman who somehow found herself giving instructions in the English language to German high-ranking soldiers, bureaucrats and spies. Heinrich Beck provided a considerable challenge as he combined Teutonic arrogance with startling stupidity. The tuition of a language to an adult was subject, not only to the intelligence of the student, but the student's knowledge of history, language, customs and country. The Dutch teacher found Beck to be an empty vessel. Nevertheless, she eventually was prepared to provide him with the certificate that would enable him to travel on behalf of his country. She justified her decision by saying to herself, 'I will not have to see the bastard again.'

Goebbels gave Beck his orders.

'I want you to go to London on my behalf. The British newspapers continue to spew anti-Reich propaganda. You are to go to the Embassy as my personal representative to express my dissatisfaction. Put a bomb under them', he paused, 'not a real bomb, a verbal bomb'

Heinrich Beck was excited by the prospect. He would have the opportunity to suss out the Wagner family history. He would look for skeletons – perhaps even Jewish skeletons.

He travelled to London by Luft Hansa and was met by an Embassy driver in a British Morris sedan.

'I thought you would be in a Mercedes Benz', he commented to the driver.

'It would be pelted with eggs', the driver replied, 'we are not well liked in London'.

He was greeted at the Embassy none too warmly and housed in a tiny bedroom next to the boiler system.

'You will get used to the noise', the housemaid said before she cursorily left. He could hear the gurgling, belching boiler as it struggled to keep the draughty old Embassy heated through the miserable English winters. Heinrich saw no insult in his accommodation. He rarely travelled anywhere. He did not appreciate every subtle nuance from a diplomat was designed. Artfulness was the tool of an attaché. An hour later an equerry called for him. Heinrich was taken to a large suite of offices. There were three men waiting for him. It would have been clear to most people that the diplomats were simply humouring Beck.

'We are so glad you are here, with the imprimatur of Minister Goebbels no less. We hope you will take the time to see the city. We suggest you keep a low profile. Germans are not well regarded these days. Since the Olympic Games things have got worse. We suggest you call yourself a Swiss German. They are tolerated. Now you will probably ask 'what are you fellows doing about it? We expect you will form your own conclusions and with that in mind we have made an Embassy car available for you. See the city take in the sights. Find out for yourself.'

Heinrich Beck had wondered how he would explain his real purpose, the one he kept to himself. Here was the opportunity served up on a silver platter.

'Excellent', he replied, 'is Whitechapel close. This is a place I want to visit'.

The diplomats happily explained it was nearby, 'Your driver will take you there.'

After he left, the diplomats pondered on Heinrich's request. 'Do you think he wants a prostitute, our Embassy Tarts are better quality and not crab infested', said one. 'Perhaps it is the Victorian architecture he is interested in', said the second. 'Sherlock Holmes, he is a Conan Doyle fan', said the third. They soon lost interest in Heinrich Beck and went back to discussing travel allowances and the prospect of being posted to warmer and safer places. 'Do we have an Embassy in Barbados?' asked the junior trade commissioner. 'I suggest Rio,' replied the press co-ordinator.

Beck walked aimlessly around Whitechapel asking anybody he met if they knew a girl named Sarah Green. Sarah Greengrass heard of his presence. Little happened in Whitechapel without the locals being apprised. It was not the hellhole it was in the 19th Century but there was still contraband on sale. Greengrass phoned Parrott. He was firm, 'tell him all you know, put him out of his misery.'

Sarah Greengrass approached Heinrich in a sad cafe where he was lunching. 'I hear you are looking for Sarah Green'.

'How did you know.?

'Never mind that, you are in Whitechapel now', Sarah Greengrass replied, 'she was a Jewish girl, the daughter of a tailor who moved to Cheam'.

She gave the almost panting Heinrich Beck the whole story. She even embellished it by describing the alleged piety of the girl. 'As Jews go, she was a special one. I heard she went to Europe. That's where you come from. You may have run into her.'

Beck could not wait to get back to the Embassy.

'Did you have an interesting tour'? One of the diplomats asked.

'The Reich Minister will be pleased with my work', Heinrich Beck replied.

The diplomats spoke to the driver who told them that Beck walked the streets of Whitechapel speaking to people. He described Sarah Greengrass. 'They talked for some minutes. Beck jotted in a notebook'.

The diplomats discussed the odd behaviour but were interrupted by an enquiry as to the propriety of serving lobster tails in Gruyere sauce at a forthcoming state dinner in honour of the Moroccan Ambassador. They lost interest in the travels of Heinrich Beck.

Meanwhile Beck planned for his trip back to Berlin. He was looking forward to adding to his chronicle and the eventual denunciation of the barber.

Meanwhile in Berlin Dr Karl Merz sat nervously across the desk from Dr Goebbels. The Minister was flanked by advisers. One was a Treasury man and Dr Merz felt the official was scrutinising him critically. Some of his expenses would not stand up to even a cursory audit. The costs of his trip to the Lausanne conference with a young animal behaviourist would collapse under even a minor probe. The suite at the Angleterre Hotel would give the game away.

'What about mental aberrations Merz? Can your surgery improve reasoning and logic'.

'It depends on the nature of the disability. If a brain lacks power and substance, we cannot do much if anything. A person's brainpower is governed by the number of cells possessed. We only use a fraction of our brains, and we can improve knowledge by learning and memory by training. Frankly a dumb person will remain dumb. The Swiss and Russians are working on curing or minimising mental disability in certain types of case. There is a disease called Autism that has been discovered by Dr Asperger in Vienna. It involves a person having a closed in personality. People who were diagnosed with schizophrenia are now being shifted into what Asperger is calling 'the spectrum of autism'. Often one can diagnose the disability from speech patterns. If a person cannot converse logically, shifts topics randomly or makes odd statements this may denote autism'.

'Can anything be done to rectify such a disease? If a person has skills but shows signs of autism can this be cured'? asked Goebbels.

Dr Karl Merz weighed up the question. He knew very well that so far, his attempts to shift the brain lobes of monkeys had been an abject failure leading to temporary anguish followed by an unpleasant painful death. Still, in the interests of the discipline, without funding there would be no advances in science, no alleviation of pain and no cures.

'One cannot guarantee the disease can be cured but there is a prospect that there may be a successful outcome. We would be breaking new ground. I will, of course, consult with Dr Asperger before embarking on a real-life experiment'.

'Excellent', said Goebbels.

Dr Merz left the meeting relieved that his funding would remain intact. The vexed question of the establishment's finances was not raised by Goebbels, and he was not asked about his experiments on Gipsy brains. He had lobotomised several gypsies and the victims of the operation were left as vegetables. He had with him a photo of a gypsy's brain that was deformed and misshapen. If asked he was ready to produce the photo to show the inherent shortcomings of gypsy brains. He would not mention the fellow had been struck by a piece of road paving hurled at him by an unfriendly villager and was admitted to hospital with an already distorted brain.

When he returned to the Academy he called a staff meeting.

'Our funding remains in place,' he announced to rousing applause.

21
BERLIN

Throngs of people gathered at the Tiergarten picnic ground. It was a bright sunny early Autumn Day, and early Autumn saw Berlin at its best. Students walked arm in arm, sometimes four or five abreast laughing and talking loudly. Old couples sat at park benches eating lunch and feeding the birds.

Mutte watched the scene from a picnic table under an Elm tree. Larry Cromarty secured it by arriving early. He fought off a family of Bavarian tourists for the table. When he muttered 'Nazi General's function' they hurriedly backed off. It had become something of a ritual for the group. Ronnie Tolar was an unlikely friend of Sarah Wagner having briefly worked as a waitress at the Bluttenblatt café. Though she was tardy and at times a little grubby the two found they were kindred spirits. They had playful senses of humour and well-honed deception detectors. When a minor clerk at one of the nearby embassies passed himself off as a vice-ambassador the two women smiled at one another and pretended to humour the puffed-up young man. When he left, they hugged one another and laughed uproariously.

'He is no more a diplomat than you are a virgin', laughed Sarah, 'nor Goebbels is a movie heart throb', Ronnie replied.

They stopped laughing. Even the mention of a Nazi boss was enough to cause a person to wonder and worry.

Mutte huffed mightily as she watched a group of Hitler Youth march down the park walkway. They travelled at a fast clip and other walkers hastily moved out of their way. They sang lustily. It was one of the new patriotic military songs. It was claimed Hutler wrote the words. If he did, he was no librettist. Kurt Weill would not have felt threatened. The lyrics were gauche.

> *We march like giants across the dales*
> *Our Soldiers strong and lusty males*
> *We rule the world with truth and power*
> *And our conquered squeal and cower'.*

Mutte continued to watch the men march away as their voices mingled with the other sounds of the park, the chirping birds, barking dogs and the hubbub of familial conversation.

'They say Hitler himself was the composer', said Ronnie.

'I am not surprised', said Mutte, 'it suits those idiots. I cry for Germany. My husband was a patriot, but he was a brave and honest man. The Germans were proud and warlike, but these young fellows are peanuts. My guess is they are only brave when together. I pity this country if those dunderheads in the Chancelry lead us into war. It will be the end of us,'

Her daughter-in-law looked around in concern, but there was nobody within earshot.

'Settle down Mutte, we still have Liverwurst from Rogacki, and I have a bag of cup cakes made by Frau Terbell. I have even got hold of a bottle of Alsace Riesling'.

Mutte quietened down and Sarah Wagner set the table and laid out the plates.

'We will invade France and England but that will be after we conquer Poland', Tom Wagner made this pronouncement in his usual bland manner.

'What are you saying', said Mutte, 'where did you hear this nonsense?'

'I heard Himmler and Hitler talk about it. A man called General Rommel has drawn up plans. Germany is not ready yet, but armaments are being secretly stored in bunkers. Rommel has given Hitler a paper'.

Ronnie Tolar and Larry Cromarty had been reading the International News Bulletin, a weekly English paper. They laid it down and took interest in the conversation.

'Tell us what you heard Tom?' said Larry.

'When I cut their hair, they seem to believe I am not there. I am busy with my scissors and clippers. I am not interested in what my customers say. I do not try to listen. I have a very good memory. Mutte says I am a camera.'

'That is what Christopher Isherwood called himself,' Larry exclaimed.

'I do not know him, is he a homosexual like you,' Tom replied, so loudly, a group of elderly picnickers at the next table looked over at them.

Tom changed the subject. He did not do so because he had no more to say. His mind simply shifted direction.

'Swans must have very long gullets. They must be careful what they eat. They can easily choke'.

Sarah Wagner knew it upset Tom if his current train of thought was interrupted.

'That is why Swans only eat tiny morsels', she replied.

'They eat all the time', said Tom, 'now I know why. Thank you, mother'.

The next table lost interest and went back to their cold schnitzel and potato salad.

Ronnie could see Larry Cromarty was bursting to speak. She knew he wanted to tell Sarah of Tobias Fox's visit. She placed her hand on his arm.

'Not now', she intoned.

Heinrich Beck watched the group from a clump of rhododendron bushes in the centre of the grassed area. He was using binoculars, but the Wagner table was too far away to allow him to overhear their conversation. An elderly woman was observing him closely. She came up behind him and began calling out loudly.

'Pervert scum, hiding and watching, hiding and watching, pervert scum'.

Heinrich extricated himself and scurried away still pursued by the woman. A small crowd watched the scene.

'That looks like Heinrich Beck', said Tom, 'he works in the Chancelry. He is very rude to Poppy. I do not cut his hair. It would be better if I did as he has a full head of thick hair. I could shape it with a centre part'.

The picnic finished with the group vowing to meet again soon.

Later that day Larry Cromarty sat on his bed in the apartment and opened a beer.

'What will become of us Ronnie', he said.

She shrugged. 'I will phone my German lover. Perhaps he has forgiven me.'

'I will tell the barman at The Lady Windermere that I want to see Harry Lime'.

They languished. Neither Larry Cromarty nor Ronnie Tolar had the funds to leave Berlin nor, for that matter, the connections. They lay together in their flat gently weeping in fear of their fate.

Then two days later, as if by magic, Harry Lime appeared at the rooming house. He was dressed in his usual black suit and a black overcoat that was so long it could have graced a Russian General.

Harry Lime looked around the room, taking in the unmade beds, unwashed crockery and general dishevelment.

'Get hold of yourselves,' he said to Ronnie and Larry, 'there is work to be done.'

Sarah had pondered over the remarks her son made at the picnic. Though she detested all that Lancet stood for, she was still, at heart, an Englishwoman.

She rang the London number she had been given by Lancet. He heard her out, as she told him of Tom's account of Hitler discussing the Rommel document.

'Thank you, Mrs Wagner,' he replied blandly, 'you confirm what we already know, but it is always comforting for there to be corroboration.'

22

LONDON

The streetlights on The Strand were flickering their muted yellow glow giving the street a strange sepia tone. Oliver Lancet spent the afternoon at his club lunching with Churchill. He avoided alcohol but this did not stop Winston from drinking Mumm champagne before lunch, a Haut-Brion with the duck and a glass of club sauternes with his blue cheese and coffee.

Later that afternoon when Lancet arrived at 10 Downing Street, he carefully checked that his tie was straight, and his pocket hank was angled correctly. He was ushered upstairs and straight into the PM's lounge.

'Come in Oliver', said Baldwin, 'it is nice to see you'.

They sat on uncomfortable antique French chairs that were part of the lounge suite situated in a corner of the room. Lancet wondered if they were deliberately designed to ensure the brevity of meetings. He had no liking for the French. 'About as practical as their gunboats', he thought, remembering the wide-bodied launches that tended to capsize in calm seas during the first World War.

Stanley Baldwin was, as usual, seeking to appear convincing.

'Hitler assures me he has no plan to invade England. He looked me straight in the eye. I believe I am a good judge of character. I find myself trusting the fellow. I have always liked you Lancet. We have had our differences, but I know you are a man of honour. Am I being naïve?'

Oliver Lancet was imperturbable.

'I am afraid, PM, you are asking me a political question. I am not apprised of hard evidence. I have a man in Berlin. He is undercover as an Embassy official. I will inform him of your concern. It is time, perhaps, he was brought home. I will put him at your disposal. He is the Johnny-on-the-spot as it were'.

Baldwin expressed his gratitude, and Lancet went back to the Cage. He contacted a very chuffed Bill Masterson.

'The Prime Minister has personally asked for you. He wants your advice. It is time you came back to Blighty. You must be sick of Turnip soup and Bear casserole'.

Masterson was not sure what Oliver Lancet was talking about. He had never been offered Turnip soup and, as far as he knew, Germans had no liking for Bear meat. But to be personally sought after by Baldwin now that was an honour.

When he returned to London, he was summonsed to Downing Street and re-assured Baldwin that Hitler was a man of honour, and his cabinet were gentlemen. Herman Goring's propensity to wear garish lipstick and rouge he dismissed as a harmless idiosyncrasy. The PM introduced him to the rag tag bunch of sycophants, toadies and gormless humbugs who were his remaining parliamentary supporters.

'We have nothing to fear', Masterson told them, 'Hitler is looking West, but the land he wants is populated by German speakers. He is only interested in restoration of the Prussian Empire'.

The Cabinet lapped it up. Masterson was appointed special adviser on Foreign Affairs to the Government and Lancet happily agreed to his transfer from the Secret Service to the Office of the Prime Minister. He sent Parrott to Berlin as his new agent. He was impossible to hide under the cloak of a diplomatic posting, and he was appointed Head of Embassy Security.

Lancet went to see Churchill. 'I have killed a murder of crows with one stone Winston. I expect in a few weeks you should have a clear run'.

Churchill puffed on his cigar. 'I will ready the hounds and fatten the beast.'

Lancet enjoyed and was used to obscure conversation. It was, after all, his stock in trade. He said his goodbyes and returned to the Cage.

Bill Masterson charmed the Cabinet.

'I have a contact in Vienna. He conducts an export-import business. We should perhaps establish a relationship with him. There is a demand these days, perfectly unnecessary mind you, for black-out curtains. He can supply them. I suggest you grant him an import licence. This will establish our bona fides. He will keep us informed of any developments in the Reich Ministry. He has impeccable contacts.'

And so it was that the UK bought a shipload of black-out curtains from Harry Lime.

23

BERLIN

When Heinrich Beck perused his Tom Wagner dossier, he realised that the document was a double-edged sword. In the first place his investigation was totally unauthorised. Secondly although he found evidence Wagner was likely part Jewish there were rumours that Goebbels and even the Fuhrer were also not devoid of Jewish ancestors. He also knew the Barber was well liked, even cosseted a bit in the Chancelry because of his great skill combined with his eccentric manner. Then there was Poppy. She would denounce him. She would claim he was obsessed by his investigation. She would say he spent his days hanging around the salon. She may even claim he ogled her. He could deny this but then may have to admit his sexual preference was to be spiked by sweaty, hairy male subalterns. He put the dossier in his desk drawer.

Tom Wagner, in the meantime, was directed by a note from, no less than Goebbels himself, to attend the Chancelry Clinic. He was not sure why, but Poppy, to alleviate concern, told him it was probably a routine check-up.

'It gives the lazy doctors something to do to earn their keep.'

Tom went happily enough to the clinic. The nurses usually treated nothing more than stomach upsets, caused by too much pilsener, or the odd case of crabs caught by unwary young officers in the fleshpots of Fredrich-Shain. Doctors came on call and there was a direct phone line to the city ambulance service. The resident nursing staff were honoured to have the famous Doctor Merz attend the clinic. Not only was he present but dressed in a white coat with a stethoscope around his neck and followed around by a bevy of assistants with notebooks wheeling trays of equipment.

Dr Merz saw Tom in one of the consulting rooms where visiting doctors saw employees of the Chancelry. His accompanying staff hung around the back of the desk taking notes and hoping and waiting for further instructions

'Tell me about yourself Tom', asked the Doctor, in his best insincere bedside manner. Merz was solely a research scientist. He had no empathy for other humans.

'I am not sure what you want to know Sir; I am a men's hairdresser. a barber, I have a very fine set of scissors and clippers. I soak them every evening in boiling water. I then clean them with a chamois and use brine to make them shine. I have a new brush. I was told the bristles are badger hair. I saw a badger one day when we went to the Grunewald for a picnic. The animal had a black and white neck. I disturbed it when I was foraging for mushrooms. You must be very careful when collecting mushrooms. Some varieties are dangerous. The badger was angry when I walked near him. He would be very angry if you pulled out strands of his hair. I am glad I am not a badger hair collector'.

Tom finished speaking and began playing with his hands. He was nervous. He was not sure why he was being interviewed by the doctor. Tom knew that when he was nervous, he babbled more than usual. Mutte often said, 'don't jibber-jabber Tom, think before you speak'. Today he was nervous, and he was 'jibber jabbering.'

Dr Merz watched Tom Wagner carefully and made notes on his yellow ruled pad. This only made Tom more nervous.

'My Mutte tells me I should be more careful when I speak, she says I prattle like a chucklehead. I am not sure what a chucklehead looks like. I saw an eagle on the roof of the fire station on Sunday.'

'Do you find cutting hair a rewarding job Tom'. Doctor Merz was pleased. He already concluded there was something wrong with the young man. He blathered like a coot.

'The pay is good. I have a driver, and I can afford to take my mother and Mutte for dinner sometimes. Poppy is a good friend'.

Dr Merz was getting used to Tom's sudden changes of direction.

'Poppy she is your assistant. Do you have a romantic interest in Poppy'.

'I don't think so', Tom Wagner replied obliquely.

When Tom left, Dr Merz summonsed Tom's driver. He was helpful.

'The fellow is very nice to me, but he talks funny'.

Poppy was less amenable.

'I don't know what your game is, but there is nothing wrong with Tom Wagner. He is a kind man and a brilliant barber'.

She added, 'he makes more sense than most people around here'.

She waved her arms as if to encompass the whole Chancelry

When Goebbels conferred later with Dr Merz he was encouraged.

'The young man suffers from a rare and new brain disease called autism. In some cases, it can be cured by an operation. The lobes may be displaced or out of sequence. It requires a lengthy procedure. I will open his head and make whatever adjustments are necessary. I will consult with Dr Hans Asperger, the great young Viennese doctor, to see if he will come to Berlin to assist me in the operation'.

'We will, of course, need the young man's approval', said Dr Merz.

'I will make him a Lieutenant in the Army. He will then be bound to obey orders.'

"Excellent', Dr Merz replied, 'then this only leaves the question of funding. We are stretched very thin at the Institute. The operation I propose is but the first step. If it is successful then it will become necessary to employ more staff, invest in surgical equipment and consult with World luminaries in the field.'

'Put in a claim and you will be paid', Goebbels replied.

Tom Wagner was surprised to be made a Lieutenant in the Army.

'You will not be required to wear a uniform. The Cabinet wishes to recognise your good work'.

Sarah Wagner and Mutte were excited by the appointment, but Poppy was not so sure 'beware of Nazis bearing poirboire', she said mixing her languages and metaphors.

Later Dt Merz phoned Dr Asperger and told him of his plans. The great Viennese physician was scornful.

'You are mad Merz, the disability is neurotic or mental. I treat sufferers with curative education. Brain lobes are not bloody chess pieces. You cannot just shuffle them about. I want nothing to do with it.'

24

SCOTLAND - BERLIN

Tobias Fox did not often visit Dundee. He found the city disturbing. The wind whistled through the streets as if it was sounding the arrival of a revenant. Tree branches swayed and leaves were torn off and flew like paper planes around the parks and sidewalks.

Since his return to Islay his pain at the loss of Sarah and the perfidy of Lancet barely eased. It was the need to tend the great vat in the distillery that kept him standing. There were occasions when the rage befell Tobias, when a bottle and a night of weeping and shouting overtook him. Then the next day he was back at work pouring and blending. The brothers coaxed him gently and the labourers stayed well clear.

He heard of a new source of sweet barley and came to Dundee to make a purchase. The information incorrect, and Tobias was consoling himself with a dram of whisky in a pub that nestled in the lee of the railway station.

He sat in a corner of the cupboard bar nursing his drink when, out of the shadows, a burly figure in black appeared. Harry Lime made himself comfortable.

Tobias was unsurprised. Spies and black marketeers often seemed to appear and disappear at will.

'Hello Harry', said Tobias Fox, 'I would not have thought Dundee was up your alley'.

'I came specially to see you Tobias'.

'I suppose I should ask how you knew I would be in this wee city, but there is no point'.

'You are right', said Harry Lime, ordering a tot of Navy Rum, 'you should not ask'.

The two men sipped their drinks in silence. Harry Lime pulled out a large gold fob watch. 'Your train is on time, Tobias, you should be getting away'.

'I am a dram away from leaving', he replied and set his glass up for a refill.

'Berlin will become a dangerous place for foreigners,' said Harry Lime.

'Lucky I am not there', Tobias replied.

'The Wagner family may need your help. In fact, the old crowd at The Lady Windermere will all need a lift out of the country'.

'You are best equipped for that job Harry.'

'Not necessarily Tobias, I think your talents will be needed. I hear young Wagner has been selected by Goebbels for some ghastly operation. My sources tell me that a doctor is going to open his noggin and shift his brain cells around'.

Tobias Fox put his glass down.

'Are you serious Lime'?

'Lime is it now? Yes, Fox I am serious. He has been made a German Army officer for no other purpose than to ensure he has no right of refusal. He has been drafted because of his disability. His mother does not know and will not be told.'

'But why Tom?'

'Because he has a minor disability and the vile Dr Merz has said he is an ideal subject to practise is dark art upon. Merz has burned money and is using Tom as a means of raising more funds from Goebbels.'

'That is all fine and dandy Harry Lime but why me?'

'You know why! And in return you shall arranged to remove Rommel's war plan from Hitler's office'.

'In return for what? What are you talking about? I have never heard of this plan.'

"It is what I am paying for. The travel for all is on me Tobias. Even a driver and nurse will be on hand. When you have the document meet me in Vienna'.

Harry Lime handed Tobias an envelope containing a thick wad of Sterling and walked out of the bar.

Tobias Fox travelled back on the train to the distillery. There was no saloon on the train, but he bought a bottle of whisky at the pub on his way to the platform. When he returned home, he fell into a drunken stupor. The brothers read the signs. 'He will be off in the morning', said one and the other agreed.

They were correct. On the following morning Tobias returned to Berlin.

The city was quiet. People huddled on corners whispering to each other. The cabarets were open but the spruikers outside seemed subdued and forlorn. The Lady Windermere was closed – 'for renovations'. The sign on the door claimed.

Tobias went to the flower shop. Sarah Wagner was not there. The shop was manned by an earnest young fellow who was eager but disorganised.

'Where is Sarah? I am an old friend. I am visiting from Scotland'. Tobias spoke in German.

The young fellow answered in English. He spoke in the American twang of cowboy country – Texas or Arizona, Tobias guessed.

'She is out for the day. She has some appointments. I fill in for her. I am a visiting student'.

Tobias thought 'as if I could not guess.'

'My name is Tobias Fox. I am a friend of the family from Scotland. Could you ask her to ring me? It is urgent and relates to the welfare of young Tom. I am at the Adlon'.

Tobias went back to the great hotel. He generally preferred the pensione, but the anonymity of the massive hostelry suited his present needs.

He was phoned by the front desk at twilight.

'A lady is here to see you Mr Fox, a Mrs Wagner'.

Tobias found Sarah Wagner seated in an alcove in the lobby. He gestured and she rose and followed him into the large lobby lounge. He ordered coffee.

'I was looking for you today, Sarah. I wanted to explain my circumstances'.

'It would not have mattered Tobias', she replied, 'God knows what you wanted from us. I am a florist and my son cuts hair. He works close to the Cabinet office, but he has no access to state secrets. I suspect you were prepared to trade on his innocence. You were placing my family at risk – great risk. I thought you were a decent man. I even thought we may have a future together. I was fond of you Tobias, you let me down. Tom is fragile. He may not look it, but he lives on the edge. He loved you Tobias and you let him down. As for me, I just feel foolish. I was taken in by a bloody spy,'

Sarah paused and sipped her coffee. She had seemed to forget why she was here.

'I understand and I have no excuse but sometimes crisis makes for strange --------.' Tobias stopped himself. He was going to say 'bedfellows' but realised it was indecorous. He substituted 'companions.'

He continued. 'I have information that Tom has been conscripted into the army. This was not a reward for his good service. It was a ruse. Now he must obey all orders. Goebbels has joined with a Dr Karl Merz to organise experiments in Eugenics. Poor Tom is to be a guinea pig'.

'Poor Tom', Tobias repeated, he remembered 'Poor Tom' was a sweet style of whisky. He blended a vat only a few months ago. His mind returned to the human Poor Tom.

'What are you talking about Tobias? Dr Merz is well respected. Tom has told me about his meeting with him. The Doctor has arranged for Tom to be treated at his clinic. He may be able to cure Tom's condition. Why are you claiming Tom is to be a guinea pig.? Is this another of your tricks?'

'No Sarah, this is no trick. Dr Merz is a Eugenicist. He is proposing to operate on Tom. He is going to shift his brain lobes around. The man is a monster. Goebbels is funding the operation. The reason Tom was commissioned was to ensure his co-operation. Your son is an innocent.'

Sarah gulped air. Though she was distrustful of Tobias, every tingling nerve of her body was telling her that he was speaking the truth. She was overcome by her maternal instinct to protect her son.

'What can we do? How can we stop the operation?'

Tobias Fox was relieved. He leant in towards her.

'You may have some leverage through your late husband. He was a War hero'.

'I am Jewish Tobias; any advantage I have from my marriage is lost if the Nazis find out. But you know that. You forget Oliver Lancet was the person who informed me of my plight. He sought to frighten me, and he succeeded. He made it implicitly clear that he may ask for my assistance and left me with an underlying foreboding. He is your superior.'

Tobias did not immediately reply. He made no admission.

'What did he want? I swear I was not aware of this. I am being used too. It is the game Lancet plays. I am just a foot-soldier.'

Sarah was watching him closely. She seemed to be less guarded, less angry.

'He left it in the air. It was suggested I would know when help was required, but surely you must know this. You are in his employment.'

Tobias thought this over. 'As usual Lancet was insulated from failure. He threatened Sarah to ensure co-operation and made her realise I was a tool of the organisation. However, Lancet would not have reckoned on Goebbels appropriating Tom for a medical experiment. This changed the game.

He took Sarah's hand

'We must find a way to save Tom from the surgeon's knife. That is the first concern. For reasons you do not need to know the only way we can then safely leave Berlin is if we get Tom to help perform a task within the Chancelry'.

'Help perform a task', Sarah's voice rose, 'what do you want him to do? He is a gentle soul. He could not hurt anybody'.

'It is nothing like that Sarah. I have yet to work out the details, but Tom's role will be passive'.

'The treatment is scheduled for next Wednesday evening'.

'You should do nothing unusual. You must act normally. I doubt that you are under official surveillance. There is an idiot clerk, Heinrich Beck, who for some reason is carrying out a private investigation of Tom. I believe him to be motivated by jealousy. Ignore the fellow. I have plans for him'.

When Sarah left the hotel in a taxi Tobias watched carefully. He could see no sign of Heinrich Beck. The dolt would have stood out like a beacon in the Adlon lobby.

On the next day Tobias rang the Chancelry.

'Can I leave a message for General Hoeven please. It is his dentist. I have a vacancy this afternoon at 3pm.'

The two men met. Hoeven had designated the place.

'Emergencies only, Fox, I am in place to operate during the forthcoming war. Your task is important to English politics, but Lancet has made it clear, and I agree that I must retain my cover. I am not going to steal any documents or send any stolen reports to Britain'.

"I understand General. However, I need to know if there really is a document from General Rommel devising a war plan and if there is such a document where it is kept. I will do the rest.'

'There is a document all right - I saw it yesterday', Hoeven replied, 'Hitler waved it around at our General Staff meeting in his office. It was on his desk in an envelope marked 'Top Secret Rommel's Advice'. Hitler apparently inspects it frequently'.

'And his office security'?

'The front door of the building is manned 24 hours by two guards, but Hitler's offices are unguarded. They house the cabinet suites, the hair salon and the boardroom'.

Tobias Fox wrote in a small notebook.

'Who would be in the Ministry Offices at 8pm'.

'Everybody or nobody – it depends. Next Wednesday evening we are all going to Spandau Citadel to watch a display of aerobatics. The whole Cabinet will be there. Goebbels has organised the International Press to be on hand to observe German pilots show their brilliance.'

'Would it be odd if the Barber organised an early evening haircut – say at 7.00pm on Wednesday Would it be even odder that this was the very evening he was to be hospitalised.'

'Not at all', the General answered, 'it would be seen as very industrious. As far as the rest of your plan is concerned you will need access cards. I guess you know that. But the Barber has an assistant, a young woman, where does she fit in'?

'Depending on the extent of her feelings for Tom I guess she either lives or dies', Tobias answered as he rose to leave the park.

25

BERLIN

The central city of Berlin was becoming an odd combination of empty silence fraught with fear and the clatter of rampaging Hitler youth in their menacing uniforms. Even in the coldest weather they wore their shorts proudly as they noisily strutted the streets. They used their sticks or now, in some cases, actual rifles to bang on walls and break windows as they marched and scrawled graffiti with thick ink pencils on any shop they deemed Juden.

The Lady Windermere remained shut. Heinrick Beck turned up one evening and studied the sign on the door.

'It looks like it has had its day', said Larry Cromarty who suddenly appeared out of the gloom and stood next to Back.

Along came Ronnie Tolar.

'I have never met you, but I have seen you at the Club. I am Ronnie Tolar'.

Heinrich Beck was exhilarated to be greeted so warmly by Larry and Ronnie.

'I have seen you many times. You have a very fine voice. I am Heinrich Beck I am an adviser to Minister Goebbels'.

'You are an important man, I knew it. I could tell as soon as I saw you'. Ronnie exclaimed.

'Those people who were with you at the end table. I take it they were old friends.'

'Not at all', Larry Cromarty replied, 'Ronnie attracts humans like blood attracts mosquitos. When you are the singer the hoi polloi likes to meet you. Of course, Harry Lime is well known. He is a mystery man, but he is good company and has a full wallet'.

'You also seem friendly with Tom Wagner'

'The barber', Ronnie said, 'not really – I know his mother. I used to work in her café occasionally but the son he hardly ever speaks. It is tricky to become friends in silence'.

'It is rather cold Heinrich. We have whisky at our home. It was given to us by a famous whisky distiller. We met him at the Lady Windermere. Come home with us and we can share a bottle.'

Heinrich Beck was not used to being treated warmly. He was not sure why it was, but people tended to regard him with either suspicion or contempt. These two Anglos were inferior to him. He knew that fact. On the other hand, they were popular habitues of The Lady Windermere and the girl was a fine singer. The barman once told him Larry Cromarty was a promising writer. He said he had met Isherwood. Heinrich was not sure who this Isherwood was, but he clearly was someone important.

They shared a taxi. Heinrich always made his own way to the Lady Windermere. He distrusted the pool drivers.

'I hear you are friends with Isherwood', he said to Larry.

'My goodness you are a literary fellow. Did you hear that, Ronnie? Heinrich is a man of letters. Did you meet him? He is my idol. I have followed in his footsteps. Are you also a bear'?

Heinrich weighed up his words. 'Was he a bear'? He was not sure what the man meant and did not realise that the expression referred to manly German homosexuals. 'I suppose I am a bit of a bear', he finally answered.

Larry Cromarty leaned across and kissed him lightly on the cheek.

'I figured as much', he said.

Ronnie Tolar was a little relieved. Ronnie was a girl of easy virtue. She was prepared to take a hit for her town and country, but this fellow was almost a bridge too far, with his ugly visage, revolting haircut and unpleasant manner. Larry Cromarty was welcome to him. As it turned out she played her part in the seduction. ''Hold my nose and venture forth' was Ronnie's motto.

The apartment was in its usual state of disarray. Various items of Ronnie's clothing were scattered about. There was a brassiere on the arm of a chair, a negligee lay draped on the floor, and the dining table was laden with dirty plates and glasses. Larry made a half-hearted attempt to clean up the mess while Ronnie, to Heinrick Beck's astonishment, stripped to her underwear and threw on a kimono.

'I once had a Japanese lover', she said.

Larry produced a bottle of the single malt.

'This is a special release from an Islay Distillery. The Master Distiller told me it was made from the purest water and the finest barley'.

The unlikely trio sat and drank the whisky. Heinrich had never tasted a drink like it. The smoothness of the almost syrupy liquid contrasted with the smoky heat generated from the peat. He relaxed. It may have been the whisky, or the easy camaraderie of his two new friends but Heinrick Beck felt at home.

He managed to reluctantly tear himself away to get back to his small flat in the Chancelry. He was never late for work as Goebbels was a strict taskmaster. As he lay in bed waiting for sleep, he recalled the sweet tongue kisses from Ronnie and the gentle hands of Larry that strayed -oh how they strayed. He wondered if he had found love and, if so, who with?

Back at the apartment Larry and Ronnie were finishing the bottle.

'That went well', said Larry'.

'He doesn't know if he is Claus or Clara', Ronnie replied.

On the following morning Harry Lime came to see them. It was only the second time he visited their flat.

He stood and twirled his homburg hat like a conjuror about to produce a rabbit from its innards.

'Invite Beck for a drink next Wednesday evening.'

He produced a small bottle of clear liquid from a pocket.

Add three, no more no less, drops of this to his whisky. He will be rendered unconscious for at least two hours. It probably will not kill him. Then open the window. My associates will be outside. They will be dressed as ambulance officers. My men will know exactly what to do. They will bring a stretcher and carry Beck to the ambulance that will be waiting outside. Follow and enter the ambulance. You will find clothing to dress as a doctor and nurse.

Cromarty – you will be the doctor. There will be identification cards in the pocket of each jacket. The ambulance will head to the Chancelry. My two men will enter carrying a second stretcher. You will remain in the ambulance with Heinrich Beck. My men will return with the Barber. He will be on the stretcher. You will then travel to a hospital where the stretcher containing Heinrich Beck will be taken to the second floor. It is here your thespian skills will be required. It should not be difficult as you have both often played the game of doctor and nurse. Leave Heinrich Beck with the charge nurse. Your journey to freedom will then commence'.

Heinrich Beck was no trouble. A brief phone call from Larry to his office at the Chancelry assured his attendance.

'Next Wednesday for a drink, that will be very fancy. And you have more of that whisky. I shall be there at 6.30pm'.

26

BERLIN

'You will have to leave Sarah. The next War will be terrible. I would not be surprised if Berlin was razed to the ground. Even if Hitler wins you and Tom will be either imprisoned or killed. These people are maniacs, and the crowd follows them like schaf. What is wrong with us? We are drugged by the thought of Aryan supremacy. But what about our Tom, if we don't do something he will be turned into a bloody vegetable by that witch doctor'.

Mutte was sitting with Sarah in the front room at the rear of their flat. She was puffing on a decent black cheroot and sipping her brandy. Sarah was weeping softly. Her usual courage had dissipated under the strain of the moment. The streets were now empty. Even the Hitler Youth were hiding in their bedrooms. Hitler was threatening Poland. Troops were massing. There were trucks, buses and horse drawn wagons taking jews over every border. The airports, train stations and ports were clogged by people trying to leave. Sarah wondered about her homeland. The British government seemed to be in a state of torpor.

The Americans were unenthusiastic about another war. 'What will become of us', she wondered.

'We must speak to Tom again. He must be made to understand'.

Mutte sat down with Tom several times explaining the dire consequences of war.

Tom listened closely to Mutte, but he was having difficulty sorting out priorities.

'But I like working in the Chancelry. Hitler is nice enough to me. He barks at most people. Herr Himmler is a bit rude, and I only cut Marshall Goring's hair once. He wanted me to blow wave the rear strands. This did not suit his hair. Where will we go?'

Mutte went over to Tom and grabbed his arm.

'Come with me. We will go for a stroll. You stay here Sarah'.

Mutte and Tom went out into the street and Sarah heard the clatter of their shoes as they walked away. They were gone for an hour.

When the pair returned Mutte made a pot of tea and toasted some bread over the fire. The three sat eating the toast spread with jam and cream.

'I understand Mother', said Tom, 'we must leave Berlin. Mutte showed me the empty shops and houses. She introduced me to the Widow Rosen. I knew her husband. He was killed by the Hitler Youth. They are nice to me, but they know I have a driver and that I work at the Chancelry. I am afraid that I will do something wrong. I do not want them to take you away – or you Mutte.'

Sarah Wagner was far from sure, as to what she should do, but her choices were limited. When Tobias

Fox arrived later that evening, he sat with the Wagner family and explained the plan.

'Tom you will stay at work on Wednesday for a late customer. You and Poppy will be the only people at work. It is the night of the Spandau shindig. I will be your late customer. I will be in a uniform and known as Colonel Vorster. I will go to Hitler's office on my own and find a letter that I need and leave. You will be collected by an ambulance. There will be a doctor and nurse in the ambulance. You have met the nurse and doctor. They are Ronnie, the singer, and her friend Larry'.

'But you are not a colonel, and they are not a nurse and doctor'? Tom queried.

'No, you are correct I am not a colonel, and Ronnie is not a nurse nor is Larry a doctor, but it is part of the plan. Remember we have a plan'. Tobias was wondering if he had signed a metaphorical death warrant for the Wagner family, the two young dilettantes and himself.

Mutte must have understood his concern and poured him a stiff brandy.

'It will be fine', said Tom, 'I will remember everything you said. I will go over it in my head every day'.

'I will help you remember, Tom, you can be sure of that', Mutte exuded a confidence that she hoped was not so misplaced that it would lead to their arrest and worse.

'What about Poppy? Will she be coming with us?'

This was always going to be the sticking point. Tobias knew it, so did Sarah and Mutte.

'It will not be safer for Poppy to travel with us. She will have other opportunities. Be careful to say nothing to her. It is a secret. This is most important.'

Tobias realised it was no answer, but it was the best he could do. He quickly changed the subject. He was trading on Tom's sprite-like mind shifting thought.

Mutte sensed the significance of the moment.

'You and your mother must leave Berlin Tom. You will not be safe staying here.'

'What about you Mutte?' Tom asked.

'I am not going anywhere,' she replied, 'your grandfather was a flying ace the Nazis will look after me. This is my home and it is where I am staying.'

When Tobias left the Wagner home he returned to his hotel. The following morning, he made two calls. The first was to Dr Merz' receptionist nurse.

'Hello this is Kapitan Wolter. I am ringing to arrange the admission of Herr Thomas Wagner for his cranium examination by Dr Merz. I am ringing on behalf of Minister Goebbels. He wants the operation carried out on Wednesday evening. I will arrange a secure ambulance. The patient will arrive in the early evening. Minister Goebbels will expect to see the patient at 7am on the following morning'.

The receptionist nurse was displeased. Dr Merz was an important man. She was not used to be treated in such a dismissive way.

'I will need to check with the doctor to see if this date is convenient. It is very short notice'.

'You misunderstand. I speak for Minister Goebbels. This is not a request. It is an order. Shall I tell the Minister you have queried his request'?

The receptionist nurse backtracked quickly. She was, of course, ready to assist. The hospital looked forward to the arrival of Herr Wagner.

Tobias rang off satisfied.

His next call was to Goebbels office. Heinrich Beck answered.

'Dr Merz surgery calling with a message for Minister Goebbels'.

'Yes, what can I do for you'?

'The Doctor will conduct his operation on Herr Wagner on Wednesday evening. He has arranged for an ambulance to pick up Herr Wagner at the Chancelry in the early evening. Please ensure the front door guards of the Chancelry are apprised of its arrival. He expects that the Minister will be able to see Herr Wagner from 7am on Thursday Morning'.

'Can the Minister and his trusted staff attend the operating theatre'. Heinrich Beck was looking forward to seeing the doctor slice Tom Wagner's head open.

'Though we call it an operating theatre, there is no viewing area. We do not allow students to observe this operation because it is at the forefront of Eugenic Theory. In any event it is not a public entertainment. Does the Minister know you have made this request Herr – what is your name again'.

Heinrich Beck hung up quickly..

Tobias Fox was content with his morning's work. He went to the hotel café for a Schnitzel.

27

BERLIN

Sarah Wagner opened her shop on Monday morning but let it slip that she was taking three days off commencing Wednesday afternoon.

'I am having a short vacation. We are driving to the hills.'

She gave the impression that the trip was perhaps a little improper – perhaps a tryst, perhaps a married man, even perhaps a diplomat. The customers grinned and wished her a good holiday.

The regulars discussed her excursion, over their pastries and coffee.

'Goodness, she deserves some luck in love what with her son being touched and her gruff old mother-in-law.' Said a Belgian trade envoy.

'I agree, let us hope she has met an honest man,' replied the Dutch commercial secretary, who believed herself to be a victim of the wiles of scoundrels, after disastrous affairs with a married press attaché and a BBC journalist.

The week passed slowly.

Tobias told Sarah to only bring essentials in a small bag. She would take a train to Berlin Central Railway

Station and wait in the café, with the flags hanging outside, in the square opposite.

On Wednesday morning Sarah opened her shop. She went through the motions, making coffee for the early regulars, receiving a delivery of pastries and spraying thirsty plants. She wondered what would become of them. Would they simply wither on the vines, or would they be watered?

Tom Wagner had a full day. There were many officers visiting Berlin. Most had been serving in Africa or the East. He shook his head at some of the atrocious haircuts he was asked to repair. The crew cut of a Major was so uneven that it could have been cropped by curving nail scissors. Parts were made on the wrong side, and the back shave line was often wavy or uneven. He worked assiduously all day stopping only for a brief lunch, of a sandwich, with Poppy.

'Do not work so hard Tom', she said, 'it is not your last day of work. You are not retiring tomorrow'.

Tom looked at Poppy closely. Did she know he was leaving tonight? Should he say something to her, to reassure her? 'No' he thought, 'it is a secret.' Poppy noticed Tom's disquiet. She picked up all his reactions. She knew he usually missed nuances and saw things in a structured way.

'I am joking Tom; you are strong as an ox. Today there are many soldiers in town for the show at Spandau and important meetings. They come with bad haircuts. They want to look their best when they meet their fellow officers for Schnapps in the Spandau bars. You are the wizard, turning bad hair cuts into good ones.'

Tom was relieved. 'Some of the barbers were butchers', he said, 'I have read that if one gets a bad haircut it will turn into a good haircut in three weeks. This is not correct. The longer strands grow longer, and the ugliness of the cut becomes worse'.

Poppy consulted the appointment book.

'I see we have a late booking. This is unusual. Colonel Vorster – is he important? You could have told me. I might have had a date. A handsome member of the Africa Corps may be here to sweep me off my feet'.

Poppy could see that her remark confused and worried Tom and he began fiddling with his hands and swaying a little.

'I am joking. I am all yours'.

After Poppy said the words, she realised she meant them. Tom relaxed and sipped his tea. In a minute lunch would be over, and Tom would be ministering to the needs of the next customer.

In the late afternoon Heinrich Beck sat in his office smacking his lips at the thought of the fool Tom Wagner having his head cut open. He supposed they would first shave his nut. He laughed to himself enjoying the thought of Wagner coming to work as bald as a billiard ball. The Chief Clerk put his head in the door.

'Stop daydreaming Beck I have work for you. There are some documents I want delivered to the Adlon Hotel. Colonel Burmeister is staying there. He is the subdirector of ordinance. Get Reception to buzz his room. He will come down and collect them. You can take the rest of the afternoon off'.

As he had plenty of time on his hands Heinrich Beck walked to the Adlon Hotel. This evening, he was visiting his new friends Ronnie Tolar and Larry Cromarty. He wondered if he would hug Ronnie or kiss Larry – or both. The Adlon Hotel was bursting at the seams. Officers had come from every outpost of the German Military machine to attend conferences and the air show. He queued at Reception before being greeted by a surly, overworked clerk.

'I have a packet for Colonel Burmeister. I am from the Chancelry. I represent Minister Goebbels'.

This usually stopped people in their tracks, but the harried clerk was unimpressed. Today every person checking in claimed an association with Goring, Himmler, Goebbels or even Hitler. He left the front desk and consulted a colleague. When he returned, he smiled revealing a mouth full of gold capped crowns.

'The Colonel is still at lunch in the Mahogony Room. You can leave the package with me.'

'My instructions from Minister Goebbels are clear. I am to hand the package to the Colonel'.

'Well wait then. The Mahogony Room is on the First Floor'. The clerk looked beyond Heinrich and waved over the next person in the queue.

Beck made his way to the Mahogony Room. There was a reception desk manned by the usual officious clerk. He looked Heinrich Beck over with mild distaste, focusing on his Hitler Youth haircut.

'Who are you looking for'? The clerk correctly identified that Beck was not a customer.

'I am an aide to Minister Goebbels. I have a package for Colonel Burmeister.'

'The clerk left his post and entered the restaurant. After a few moments he returned.

'His party is preparing to leave. They will be coming out soon'.

Sure enough, a group of Army Officers emerged from the restaurant. One of the men dressed in German officer's uniform, was Tobias Fox. Heinrich remembered him from The Lady Windermere. Fox walked past and though he looked in Beck's direction he showed no sign of recognition. The Reception Clerk spoke to a burly officer as he emerged. The man walked over to Beck.

'I believe you have something for me', he said.

Beck gave him the package when the officer produced his identification card. As the officer departed Heinrich Beck looked for Tobias Fox, but he was gone.

Beck sat on a chaise Lounge in the Lobby to consider the matter. 'Was the whisky salesman and friend of Ronnie Tolar and Larry Cromarty a German Officer. Worse still was he a spy?'

Beck was being observed by the reservations clerk who served him. He did not like what he saw. He ushered the doorman over.

'Ask that fellow his business. I do not like the look of him'.

The doorman spoke to Beck, asking him if he was a hotel guest. Heinrich considered raising his status with the fellow, but there were ranking officers milling around. 'How would he explain he saw an officer who looked like a whisky salesman he met in a down at heel Nancy bar?'

Heinrich Beck left the hotel. He remembered the whisky salesman was invited to join Harry Lime. Larry Cromarty and Ronnie Tolar were at Harry Lime's table. They will know who the fellow is. He probably supplied them with the whisky they drank on their first meeting. They would know!

Tobias had taken the elevator back to his room. He metaphorically kicked himself. It was clear that Beck remembered him. He knew Beck was due to meet his two unlikely co-conspirators. He hoped their wiles had so ensnared the fellow that he would place no store on the meeting. He waited an hour before he ventured down to the lobby. There was no Heinrich Beck. He seemed to have gone.

Tobias Fox, now Colonel Vorster, left the hotel in the limousine he ordered from the Transportation Section. When the vehicle arrived at the Chancelry, the driver leapt out and opened the door for him. The Staff Drivers were canny people who were quick to realise if a passenger required extra service or veneration. The driver identified Colonel Vorster as just such a man. The guards on the door took up the cue and barely looked at the identification card Tobias flashed as he passed into the spacious hallway.

He found his way to the Fuehrer's Quarters. The hallways were empty as the staff had either finished work for the day or were on their way to Spandau. Tobias pressed the bell button, and Poppy opened the door.

'I am Colonel Vorster,' said Tobias Fox.

Poppy immediately recognised him. She met Tobias Fox several times. He joined her and the Wagner family for a pleasant lunch one Sunday in a village café. She paused for a moment, but only for a moment. She did not know what was happening, but she realised Tom was expecting Colonel Vorster.

'Good evening, Sir,' she said, ushering him into the offices.

While Tobias Fox was entering the Fuehrer's inner sanctum, Heinrich Beck's taxi was dropping off its fare at the Larry Cromarty and Ronnie Tolar apartment.

Heinrich Beck was greeted warmly by his newfound friends.

'Come in Heinie', said Ronnie, calling him by a sobriquet last used by Beck's mother, 'our last bottle of single malt is waiting for you'.

'I wanted to ask you about that whisky', Heinrich replied, 'I saw a German officer at the Adlon Hotel. I was almost sure he was the whisky salesman who is your friend. I sat next to the fellow at the bar of the Lady Windermere. If it wasn't him, it was his twin brother'.

Larry and Ronnie looked at one another. 'Why had Tobias Fox been so stupid, was he trying to expose us?'

Ronnie was the entertainer; the show must go on was her ever-present rule of life.

'I doubt the Wehrmacht is recruiting Scottish whisky salesmen. All old tipplers look alike, what with their red faces and knotty noses. Anyway, our old friend is back in Scotland. Here I received a card from him yesterday.' She held up a postcard.

'You are right, tipplers all look alike.' Heinrich was not wholly convinced but he was enjoying the soft touch of Larry's hand stroking his thigh. He decided it would be time enough tomorrow to conduct further enquiries.

Ronnie poured the whisky. She ensured that Heinrich Beck's glass had an additive. Larry continued to stroke the fellow's leg, and this seemed to have settled him down.

'To a great future', said Ronnie, lifting her glass.

'To the fatherland', Heinrich Beck replied. He was nervous. It had been a testing day, and he gulped the first dram. It was enough. His head lolled back, and his eyes glazed.

Ronnie Tolar went to the front window. She opened the pane and waved. The two men in the ambulance below saw the signal.

They were both swarthy Southern Germans. The men were long-time trusted employees of Harry Lime. Each was dressed as an ambulance driver. The van was stolen outside a hospital, an hour before, and bore the lights and signs of a city ambulance. The rear door was opened. Inside were two portable rollaway stretchers, The two men, bearing a stretcher, left the van and hurried to the front door that was opened by Ronnie. They climbed the stairs and entered the apartment. Heinrich Beck was out to the world. He was loaded onto the stretcher, and the two men carted him down the stairs followed by Ronnie Tolar and Larry Cromarty. The Professor and his wife on the first floor peeped out from a partly open door.

'A drop too much', said Larry as he passed the landing.

Beck was loaded into the ambulance, followed by Ronnie and Larry.

'Get changed', said one of the swarthy Harry Lime employees.

Ronnie and Larry changed clothing as the ambulance set off to the Chancelry. Ronnie was provided with a nurse's uniform and Larry with the white coat of a doctor. They huddled in a corner of the van. Heinrich Beck lay prone on a stretcher and next to it was its twin, presently unoccupied.

The ambulance was expected at the Chancelry. Heinrich Beck saw to that. When one of Harry Lime's men rang Goebbel's office that day, to confirm, Beck took the call.

'An ambulance will be arriving to pick up the barber Wagner this evening. Can you make doubly sure the front door staff are informed. There must be no delay. The medical staff will be waiting in the operating theatre'

When Tobias Fox was ushered into Hitler's Offices by Poppy he was surprised at their lack of opulence. He expected Versailles chairs and Turkish ottomans. Instead, there was functional cheap wooden furniture and unpleasant brown painted walls. 'A reflection of his taste', he thought.

Poppy's mind was racing. Why was Tobias Fox impersonating a German General? What was he doing here? What did he want with Tom Wagner? Meanwhile Tobias was walking down the corridor with her – seemingly unconcerned. For his part he recognised Poppy's anguish. As they approached the salon, he murmured.

'We both love Tom, Poppy, never forget that.'

They kept walking and Poppy did not even turn her head, but she heard the whisper.

They entered the Salon.

'Hello Herr Wagner, I am Colonel Vorster. Can you freshen up my hair styling. I have been in the East'.

The family and Tobias Fox had extensively coached young Tom to pretend Tobias Fox was a German officer.

'It will not be for very long, Tom,' Tobias said to the young man, when they rehearsed his role, 'but if someone surprises us before the ambulance arrives, he has to be convinced that you are just doing your job – cutting an officer's hair.'

'And will you tell Poppy?' Tom Wagner asked.

'Leave that to me, but she must not be frightened. We do not want her raising the alarm.'

Tom Wagner was speechless. It was one thing to practise his conduct during the meeting, but now he was confronted by Tobias Fox pretending to be Colonel Vorster, it was difficult for him to keep up the subterfuge. His mind did not work in the realms of deceit or implication.

Tobias could see Tom was bothered, and he took the initiative. He removed his jacket and sat in the barber's chair.

'Just a clean up Herr Wagner. No fancy curls or shaped mutton chops. Perhaps if it is not too much trouble but I would like a a clean out of the ears. My whiskers are sprouting like new grass'.

Tom Wagner composed himself.

'Of course, Colonel, of course I will make sure that your ears are clean. If I may be so bold I would like to use my small tweezers to remove some hair from within your nostrils as well'.

'A fine idea Herr Wagner but first I have some information for the Fuehrer. Are any of his staff in his private suite'?

'They are all at Spandau or gone for the night.', said Poppy.

'I will leave him a note', said Tobias. He rose from the barber's chair and left the Salon.

Poppy confronted Tom.

'What is Tobias Fox doing here? Why is he pretending to be Colonel Vorster?'

Tom was dumbstruck. This was a hedgerow too many. He began fiddling with his scissors. He opened and shut them continuously and was half bent over. Poppy watched him. She knew the signs. He was severely distressed.

The door opened and Tobias returned. The envelope taken from Hitler's desk burnt a metaphorical hole in his back pocket.

'Sorry to keep you waiting Herr Wagner. Shall we begin'.

Tobias saw Tom was agitated and Poppy was standing with hands on hips and her jaw jutting out.

'I am acting in Tom's best interest, Poppy. God knows I love his mother. Play along. War is close at hand. I know I have done nothing to earn your trust. But this is Tom's only way out. You will have the opportunity to leave the Chancelry. Take it. In the meantime, we will continue the charade.'

Tobias sat in the chair and, as if in a trance, Poppy fitted him with a gown.

Before Tom could commence cutting, the front doorbell rang. Poppy left to answer the door. Tobias unbuttoned the apron and left the chair.

'Are you ready Tom? Our journey begins.'

Tom remembered the plan. He took off his outer garments and stood in his singlet and under shorts quietly waiting. The door opened and Harry Lime's men walked in carrying the stretcher. Poppy was walking behind them. She gave a little squeal when she saw that Tom was in his underwear and the Colonel was now out of the chair and dressed ready to depart.

Tom was laid on the stretcher under a sheet, and the two men carried the stretcher out of the salon.

'What is happening?' Poppy asked, 'where is Tom going?'

Tobias Fox gripped her by the shoulders.

'Poppy we are taking Tom to safety. He is in danger. Dr Merz is a butcher. Poor Tom would have been mutilated or killed. I know you care for him. It is better if you do not stay here. There will be a ruckus soon enough. The rear East door of the Chancelry has been left unlocked by a friend. You may care to leave with me'.

Poppy walked with Tobias Fox to the rear of the building. He opened the unlocked East door [thanks to General Hoeven]. They stepped out into the dark empty laneway.

'Good luck Poppy', said Tobias Fox. He hurried to the end of the building and climbed into the rear of the ambulance that had stopped at the curb.

Poppy watched the Ambulance disappear around the corner. She shivered but it was not from the cold, rather from a fear of what would become of her and Tom.

She stood outside the door contemplating her next move. Then she turned and briskly walked in the opposite direction to the road where the ambulance had been standing.

28

BERLIN TO VIENNA

The back of the ambulance was crowded enough before Tobias Fox entered.

'Any trouble getting him out', said Tobias through the hatch into the front compartment.

'The guards were pleased to have some entertainment,' the driver said, 'what about you?'

'None', was Tobias's reply, 'I have taken a chance with Poppy, but my gut tells me she is loyal to Tom and has no liking for nazis.'

'But she may be reporting us now,' Cromarty said.

'The alternative was to kill her,' Tobias whispered in his ear.

Larry Cromarty said no more on the subject.

Tobias changed from his uniform into a neat single breasted worsted suit. The ensemble was completed with a crisp white shirt and paisley bow tie. There was a large canvas bag in a corner. The front seat passenger opened the hatch and leaned around.

'Put your clothes in the bag and place the brick on the top of the bag. There is a nice new outfit for you too, Tom.'

Tom Wagner sat up. He noticed a bundle at the foot of his stretcher. He was provided with fresh underwear and a neat casual outfit of grey pants, navy jacket, and tan shoes.

There was a brick on the floor beside the bag. Tobias filled the bag with the clothes and brick and secured it with a knot. The front seat passenger spoke through the hatch.

'Place the bag at the rear door'.

The vehicle suddenly pulled up. The front passenger opened the rear door and took the bag, shutting the door as he left. He shortly returned to the ambulance and the journey re-commenced. He leant through the hatch.

'The fish in the Spree River will be well dressed', he said before closing the hatch.

When the vehicle arrived at the front entrance of the Berlin Brain Surgery Academy, Harry Lime's men removed the stretcher on which lay the still unconscious Heinrich Beck. Ronnie Tolar and Larry Cromarty followed, clad as medicos.

'There are some blankets in the corner. Lie under them. We will lock the back door. We won't be long', said the driver to Tom and Tobias.

The party made their way into the lobby of the clinic. The area was deserted save for a harried nurse who was pacing the floor.

'You are late', she said, 'follow me and we will get the patient prepared.'

She examined the unconscious Heinrich Beck.'

'Why is he sedated, that is the job of our anaesthetist?'

'He was nervous about the operation. He has been personally selected by Reich Minister Goebbels. He was anaesthetised on the Minister's instructions. Shall I tell the Reich Minister you question his decision.'

The nurse recoiled and, without further comment, led them into the surgical ward. Heinrich Beck was rolled onto a gurney and a team of doctors and nurses arrived and began examining him and wiring him to various sinister looking contraptions. The Harry Lime men, plus Ronnie and Larry, quietly withdrew out of the ward and returned to the ambulance.

'We have delivered the cargo. You are safe to show yourselves.'

Tobias Fox and Tom Wagner shook off their blankets and sat back on the rear bench.

'Did everything go to plan? asked Tobias.

The front passenger ignored his query and gave him a piece of notepaper. 'Read and understand the contents than eat the paper'.

The vehicle drove to the Central Railway Station. Young Tom sat silently. He began rubbing his hands and swaying. Tobias noticed and took the young man's hands.

'Relax Tom', he said, 'we are going to pick up your mother.'

The ambulance pulled to a halt and the front seat passenger leaned through the grille.

'We are at the back entrance of the café. Fox get Frau Wagner.'

Tobias went through the service entrance and walked past the kitchen. Sarah was nursing a coffee at a window table. She was watching the street. Tobias approached and sat at the table.

'Your son is waiting for you. Go back past the kitchen and through the service door. I will settle your account and follow. There is an ambulance in the laneway. Knock on the back door.'

Sarah set off past the kitchen, stopping a couple of times to look back. Tobias paid for her coffee and followed.

When the two returned to the ambulance and entered there was little room to move. The party hobnobbed around the remaining stretcher.

The front seat passenger opened the grille.

'We will get moving, it will only be a matter of time before somebody starts asking questions. Ambulances do not sit stationary outside café kitchens. You will have to change while we are in transit.'

Tobias nodded and the ambulance took off. He brought the group together. They gathered around the stretcher.

'We have instructions and more clobber from our benefactor. You will need to change clothing – in some cases again.'

He pointed to a large wicker box in a corner.

He realised, 'benefactor', was a fanciful way to describe Harry Lime. He was not sure what Lime's reward would be – but surely it would be handsome.

'Ronnie you are to be our star. You are Veronika Veronika, a famous songstress. You are travelling to Vienna to perform a series of concerts. Harry has even provided some advertising leaflets that we can distribute'.

He handed out sheets from a sheaf of paper.

VERONIKA VERONIKA
STAR OF THE FOLLIES
PERFORMING A CAPTIVATING NIGHT
OF SONG
VIENNA CONCERT HALL

There were dates provided for three concerts. Ronnie read the advertisement with an ooh and aah of pleasure.

'But I have not prepared a song list and who will accompany me? Do I have a Jazz Band and what about rehearsals?'

'The program is of no consequence, Ronnie. It is our cover. Now change into your dress and apply make-up from the kit provided.'

Tobias continued, 'As part of our performance you have been taken ill. You will be carried on board. You have caught a bug in Berlin.'

'Train, what train, where are we going'? Larry Cromarty asked.

'We are going to Vienna; it will not, of course, be our final destination.'

Tobias spoke with as much authority as he could muster. He wondered why the group was heading East when England lay West. He waved a sheaf of tickets.

'We have placed our faith in Harry Lime. It is too late to turn back. Soon enough Goebbels will find that young Tom is not the patient on the operating table.'

The group quietened and Tom was comforted by his mother.

'Tom you are the hairdresser to the star. You will be at Veronika Veronika's side cosseting her and fluffing her new blonde wig. You will find it in the hat box Ronnie'.

While Ronnie admired her spectacular arctic white wig Tobias turned to Larry Cromarty and Sarah Wagner.

'Larry you are Veronika Veronika's dresser. You shall be as camp as a boy scout picnic. This will not be a difficult task for you. Sarah you will be the trusted companion. Our star is as histrionic as she is extravagant. You two are bit players to our star'.

'What about you?' asked Sarah Wagner.

'I am the impresario.', answered Tobias Fox, 'I am already in my garb.'

The rest of the group quickly dressed in their costumes. The ambulance soon reached its destination. It was the front entrance of the Berlin Central Railway Station. Harry Lime's man got out of the front cabin and opened the back door. The strange group emerged and led by Tobias Fox climbed the stairs and entered the station. Larry and Tom were at the front and rear of the stretcher that they rolled through the main station mall. They were accompanied by Sarah Wagner who occasionally would daub the prone Ronnie Tolar's face. The lead actress played her part well. She continually complained and gesticulated as the strange troupe passed into the bowels of the station. Harry Lime's plan worked to perfection. The crowd saw a leading lady cosseted by a cast of lackeys. The individuality of the various members disappeared into the stage set of the ensemble If asked an onlooker would say, 'there was an ill star on a cot surrounded by the hired help.' They would be unable to describe the lackeys. One witness might say 'there was a manager, perhaps a director. He was an older fellow,' but there the description would lapse. Railway passengers and visitors had their own concerns. 'Was the train on time', 'is my ticket in order,' or 'how far is it to my my carriage.' The tangle of humanity had only a passing interest in the oddity of others.

The team made its way to the overnight sleeper train to Vienna. There was a crush on the platform. Tobias identified that the passengers were largely family groups. Jews were heading for the East, perhaps Rumania or Hungary. There were Nazi soldiers in the all-black uniforms of the new Gestapo Waffen SS force. They were rumoured to consist of criminals and half-wits. Tobias saw wild eyed, angry men who, for reasons unknown, bore a violent hatred towards Jews. It was a strange almost inexplicable wrath. He saw it as resentment of the success of the Jews, fuelled by cartoons of long nosed usurers and stories of scheming business practices. The failure of the moronic led to the envy of the prosperous.

The Jewish families were in orderly queues. The children were quietly sniffling and snuggling their sad mothers. The men, in their dark suits and black pork pie hats, stood holding their sheaves of tickets awaiting their turn to be interrogated. Hitler youth patrolled, clipping adults across the head if they deviated from the exact line of the queue. The tableau was one that deserved to be seen by the world.

Tobias had little time for reflection. He led the party to the First-Class front section. He waved to a train porter who came running to greet them.

'We are the Veronika Veronika party. Madame Veronika Veronika is somewhat poorly. Can you assist us to expedite our entry'. Tobias thrust a decent handful of marks into the Porter's hand.

'Sorry I have no dollars or francs', he intoned.

They entered their private compartment and were ministered to by an obsequious attendant.

'Your meals can be served here Sir, or you can eat in the dining carriage. There is a bell by the door. I will be at your service'.

The party relaxed. They settled on comfortable chairs. Tobias left the blinds open.

'We are on show. Veronika Veronika is our star. Let the people gawk. It removes suspicion'.

Sarah Wagner viewed Tobias with interest. 'The man is skilled in the black arts. Perhaps, after all, we may escape Hitler's gang, but what awaits us?' She did not know but whatever his motives she understood Tobias was a brave man. She realised she may have misjudged him.

There was a piano and stool in a corner of the sitting room of the compartment. Tom Wagner sat on the stool and opened the lid. He liked to hum the Horst Wessel song. He began striking the keys. Magically he played the song. Ronnie Tolar, already firmly ensconced in the role of Veronika Veronika came over to the piano and watched.

'I can play the piano Mother,' Tom said.

'My grandmother could play by ear. Perhaps you inherited the skill,' Sarah Wagner replied.

'I can only use my hands,' Tom said, 'I do not know how I could play by ear?'

Ronnie Tolar began singing Horst Wessel in time to Tomas' piano.

'Perhaps we can really put on a concert', posited Larry Cromarty.

'A bonus or a blunder,' Tobias Fox remarked.

29

BERLIN

After Heinrich Beck was deposited at the Berlin Brain Surgery Academy the nurses prepared him for surgery. His head was shaved and he was washed.

'The man is disgusting. His armpits smell like the inside of a bat's cave.' Said the head nurse.

The anaesthetist was fretful.

'Why is he unconscious? How am I able to detect the dosage?'

'Just keep him alive'? said the head nurse, who was used to petulant physicians.

Dr Merz arrived. He was almost sober. He came from the Spandau conference, where he had been cozying up to some of the new Eugenicists. He listened in awe as a professor of neurology from Koln explained how giant magnets could affect brain stimulation.

'A regiment of puny cowards can be transformed into a robotic war machine', the academic posited.

'Hitler can do that already by his speeches', an orthopaedic surgeon from Munich replied. There was silence. 'Was the fellow joking? Was the joke permitted?'

He reluctantly left the party, but he was energised by the knowledge that he was about to make medical history. Surely, at the next conference, he would be extolled and envied.

Merz scrubbed and entered the operating theatre. He was greeted as 'maestro', his preferred title.

The operation went smoothly. When he sliced open the skull, he was a trifle disappointed.

'Everything seems to be in place. He has a small brain. I am surprised he is perceived to be a person of intellect. I will transfer the front left lobe to the rear right lobe and move that lobe forward.'

The operation went smoothly. Heinrich was stitched up and Dr Merz left to join his transvestite Japanese lover who was waiting for him in their hideaway apartment in Charlottenburg.

During the night Heinrich Beck woke and began moaning. The night nurse kept him sedated with morphine.

Goebbels enjoyed his evening at Spandau. He dined with some of his staff. They were all suitably deferential. He was informed by the Clinic the operation was carried out on the Barber, and it had been successful. He was told he could see the patient in the morning. There was much conversation about this turn of events, and it was decided to visit the patient at first light.

On the next morning Goebbels and four of his stooges arrived at the Clinic at 7am. The Surgical Superintendent and the whole medical staff were lined up in the foyer. After the compulsory bowing and scraping and a couple of brief insincere speeches they were ushered into the wardroom where Heinrich Beck lay. His right foot was visible as the blanket had slipped, and he wore a cardboard tag bearing the name TOM WAGNER in large black print on his big toe.

The group approached the bed. Beck lay on his back. His head lolled to the side and his mouth was open. His tongue swished from side to side in an alarming manner.

'Is that the Barber,' asked a lackey, 'he looks different?'.

'His head has been shaved', said another.

Heinrich's eyes were shut but the noise of the visitors woke him. He looked around the room. His eyes fastened on Goebbels.

'Dada, dada', he said.

'That is not the Barber,' Goebbels exclaimed, 'it is my office clerk Heinrich Beck.'

Hitler arrived at the Chancelry the morning after Heinrich Beck was transformed from a dullard to an imbecile. He was later than usual as he stopped on the way to meet a deputation of welders who were seeking higher pay and better conditions. When he left, Hitler believed he had calmed them down, but the group of SS officers watching the rally may have had more to do with the union's servility than Hiter's powers of persuasion.

There was a deputation of senior staff waiting for the Fuehrer.

'Dr Merz operated on the wrong person. One of Dr Goebbels' staff has had his brain re-arranged. The Barber is gone. He has disappeared. And the girl Poppy she is also missing.'

Martin Boorman, Hitler's aide, sought to make sense of the hysteria. He called for order and carefully sorted the wheat from the chaff.

Meanwhile, the Fuehrer scuttled into his office and waited for Boorman.

Hitler was always babbling away, just below boiling point, and it was usually left for Martin Boorman to keep his desk clean, avoid disasters and sweep away the dross. Boorman was one of the few Nazis who was so tonsorially conscious he had his hair cut outside the Chancelry. He frequented Ferdie's Salon where he was a long-standing customer of the owner Ferdie Varento. He knew Tom Wagner and something of his reputation. Ferdie told him the young man was a gifted barber but was strange and awkward in company. 'Loopy' was how Ferdie put it. Boorman had also heard of Poppy.

'No' he was told, 'she was Tom's minder. She watched over him like a sister but romance I saw no sign of romance. The boy is touched'.

Martin Boorman was unconvinced. He was paid to be a keen observer and there was much to observe in the Chancelry.

He cleared the office. Hitler seemed to have forgotten the missing Barber and was contemplating plans for a new tank factory near Vienna. The plans were pinned to a wax board on the wall opposite his desk. Boorman examined the desk. Everything seemed in order. Perhaps young love was the reason for the missing Barber. Perhaps an improbable romance had blossomed.

'Where do you keep Rommel's War Plan?' he asked his Fuehrer.

'It is in the bottom drawer', answered Hitler.

Boorman looked. The plans were gone. Knowing Hitler, if he blurted out the information he would blow a fuse. His voice would be heard in Koln.

'I suggest we call in the Ministry for a meeting it appears that there has been a crisis at the Clinic. And the plan seems to have been temporarily mislaid.'

Boorman rushed away before Hitler commenced caterwauling. His boss was many things but 'measured' and 'rational' were not words that came to mind.

The Cabinet assembled in the large conference Room.

Martin Boorman laid out what he knew.

'Apparently Minister Goebbels arranged that the young Barber be operated on last night, by Dr Merz, at the Berlin Brain Surgery Clinic. Somehow an employee of Minister Goebbels named Heinrich Beck was substituted for Wagner. The operation did not go well. Mr Beck is now a vegetable. The Barber has disappeared. His assistant Poppy is also gone but I do not know if they left together. This set of mishaps would be unpleasant but not earth-shattering except for one other fact. The Fuehrer was in possession of a memorandum from General Rommel of an important and confidential nature. Most of you have heard of the report. It details a prospective war plan, it is missing'.

There was a buzz among the Cabinet.

'You say this fellow Beck is a vegetable, what do you mean, what sort of vegetable?' General Ribbentrop was a veteran of the Great War and clearly was a man of literal thought.

'No, I mean that Beck has the reasoning of a toddler'.

Ribbentrop harrumphed as if to say, 'why didn't you say so'.

'What is this plan?' Goring had always coveted the Fuehrer's job. He did not realise that his rouge, lipstick and nylon stockings were barbed wire barriers to him ever reaching the zenith. He always believed he was left out of crucial discussions and not shown important reports. He was sometimes correct. Hitler may have been crazy, but never when it came to politicking.

Hitler rose:

'I asked General Rommel to prepare a war plan for an invasion of England. It is a detailed schedule of points of entry, weak spots, men and armaments required. It is incomplete and in preliminary form. I was waiting for a more complete proposal before putting it before the Cabinet for implementation'.

This was all partly true, though Hitler had been prone to wave the report around if a Cabinet member showed any sign of weak knees.

The Fuehrer's statement momentarily quietened the men at the table, but they were restless and looked at one another with concern.

Martin Boorman remained imperturbable.

'If the Barber has taken the document we need to find him. In any event we want to know how and why Beck was substituted'.

'You say Beck has the mind now of a toddler. Can he answer simple questions', Ribbentrop had seemingly recovered from the folly of his previous questioning.

'He is limited to oohing and aahing though I understand he referred to Minister Goebbels as dada.'

'I was there when he woke. He was babbling like a baby. He was not suggesting I was his father. I am afraid we will get nothing out of him. His brain is rice pudding'.

Ribbentrop began to speak but stopped, realising that Goebbels was being euphemistic.

Martin Boorman stood and walked towards the door.

'The Fuehrer has asked me to arrange a co-ordinated investigation. It is, I suppose, possible that it is a coincidence that an important document goes missing at the same time as the Barber dissapears. I cannot fathom where Heinrich Beck fits into the puzzle. He is a mere clerk and a low-grade clerk at that. Minister Goebbels informs me he was largely used as a messenger to deliver documents to other departments. I have asked Chief Inspector Savvas Christou of the State Police Intelligence Unit to join us.'

'Savvas Christou! He sounds Greek,' exclaimed one of Himmler's Military advisers.

'His father is Greek. He is a Philosophy Professor at Koln University. His mother is Aryan. The Inspector has Classical training. He read Anglo-Saxon History at Magdalen College Oxford. He is our best man let me welcome him.'

Christou was a swarthy fellow with curly black hair and striking bright blue eyes. His body was muscular and seemed to be trying to burst from his tight black three-piece suit, He carried an unfashionable flat workers cap. He sat on an uncomfortable French Provincial chair, one of a set, hijacked from a Jewish family who were languishing in a prison camp.

The police chief inspector addressed the meeting.

'I will need to have statements taken from all members of the Cabinet. My men are waiting outside the Chancelry. We will also need to speak to the Chancelry staff. The comings and goings of Beck and the Barber are of particular importance. I understand the staff will be informed that full co-operation is required. My men will be respectful and ethical. Pistos! As the Ancients would say.'

He bowed and left the room. The old soldier Ribbentrop asked his neighbour about the remarks

'What is this pissed off', he muttered.

'Ancient Greek,' replied his neighbour.

'This whole day is Greek to me,' answered Ribbentrop.

Savvas Christou left the building and waved at a large bus parked on the opposite side of the grand entry. Thirty plain clothed detectives emerged. They were his best operatives. Included was Millie Geiger, the first plain clothed female detective inspector in Berlin's Special Division. She met Savvas Christou at Oxford University where she was also studying classics. She joined the force at his persuasion. Millie was an openly lesbian woman, and her bold ties and pin stripe men's suits caused consternation within the ranks of the 'old guard' of male detectives.

'English detectives are not nicknamed 'dicks' for nothing,' one said over Lagers at a hole in the wall bar across the road from Police HQ.

Christou and Geiger organised the detectives into small groups and the investigation began.

30

BERLIN TO VIENNA

By early evening the Veronika Veronika party was firmly ensconced in their new surroundings. Tobias Fox was a true impresario. He watched his brood like a mother hen and even reduced his consumption of whisky to a few half drams. The Train Steward left a menu with him in the late afternoon.

'Will your party be dining in, Herr, or shall I reserve an end table in the dining car.'

Tobias paused and thought before he answered. 'Would a musical company including a famous vocalist stay in their cabin?' He decided on a middle course. They would eat in the First-Class restaurant car but avoid contact with other diners.

'We will dine out, but I must insist we not be troubled by other guests. Sometimes autographs are requested, or worse people seek to join our party. I appreciate your First-Class diners are largely gentle folk but there are exceptions.'

The steward immediately agreed. He had bragged to guests in the saloon car:

'We have the famous singer Veronika Veronika onboard. I am hoping she may give us a song. She has a piano in her suite. I have heard her practice. She has the voice of an angel.'

By the time the Veronika Veronika party made its way to the First-Class Restaurant Car the other passengers were all cognisant that there was a famous chanteuse on the train.

'The great singer Veronika Veronika is onboard. She must have concerts in Vienna. I hope she gives us a recital after dinner,' said a middle-aged shrew to her husband, a furniture retailer with four shops in Austria and the wish to expand into Germany now Hitler had unified the two countries.

'Never heard of her,' he replied.

By late afternoon word spread. Though several passengers claimed either no knowledge or no interest in Veronika Veronika, by dinner time, there were many people who claimed to have attended her concerts in Berlin and there was even an SS Kapitan in steerage who boasted to have squired her to the Midsummer Ball in Utrecht and later ravished her in a suite at the Grand Hotel.

Tobias led the way to the dining carriage. The party made its way through a parade of gawking fellow passengers.

'Avoid communication,' said Tobias, 'let me do the talking'.

The meal went off without a hitch, but when they were consuming their coffee and cakes a note was handed to Tobias by their waiter.

IT WOULD GIVE US ALL GREAT
PLEASURE IF THE GREAT SINGER
VERONIKA VERONIKA SANG
JUST ONE SONG

A youngish Oberst with a flashing smile waved when Tobias read the note and looked around the dining car.

'Tom, do you think you can accompany Ronnie on the song you played in our carriage.'

'I think so,' he replied.

Tobias rose and addressed the carriage.

'Veronika Veronika has kindly agreed to sing. Fortunately, one of our crew plays the piano and can accompany her. I am afraid there will be no encores as our star must rest her voice. Travel is wearing on the larynx. As you will hear, her voice is an instrument. I give you Veronika Veronika.'

Tom Wagner sat at the piano. Ronnie rose and bowed to the crowd. She nodded to Tom, and he commenced to play the introduction. She sang the Horst Wessel Song as it had never been sung before. The crowd was hushed. Soldiers and plebs from the cheap seats crowded in the doorways. Ronnie was magnificent. Her voice was never better. When she finished there was rapturous applause and a lone voice called out VeeVee, VeeVee. She looked curiously in the direction of the cry and the boasting Kapitan said to his friends, 'it was my pet-name for her. She remembers me.'

As the applause continued Tobias gathered the group and escorted by stewards made their way back to their stateroom.

They celebrated with gewurztraminer and cheese rolls that were delivered by the steward.

Ronnie Tolar was excited and rowdy.

'Perhaps we can really do the show. Perhaps Veronika Veronika may be a shining star,' she said, 'I have even received an offer from an admirer,'

Tobias Fox pricked up his ears.

'What offer?' he asked.

Ronnie handed him a scrawled note.

'The steward gave it to me. The writer was a handsome Oberst. He waved to me. I have an admirer.'

Tobias Fox was handed the note. It read:

'YOU ARE A BEAUTIFUL WOMAN WITH
A VOICE TO MATCH. PHONE ME AT
VIENNA 202065 SO I CAN TAKE YOU TO
DINNER OBERST WERNER LOEV.'

The letter was surprisingly written in English, though Ronnie had not disclosed her nationality to the audience. However, as her German was tinged with the traces of English drawl this must have led to the officer's deduction.

Tobias read the note again:

'One never knows, the invitation may be useful.'

When the train arrived in Vienna there were two familiar faces. Lime's ambulance drivers had made it to Vienna. The party was ushered into a black Mercedes bus and without comment they were taken to central Vienna. Two blocks from the Sacher Hotel there was a side street lined with small hotels. Each had a red awning and a distinctive sign. When they stopped outside the Hotel Glock they noticed there was an elderly woman waiting on the steps. As they alighted the woman came forward and handed Ronnie a red furry toy bear.

'Welcome to my hotel', she said and kissed Ronnie on the cheek.

'I am Madame Glock. I am at your service'.

The woman examined the group.

'And you must be the impresario,' she said to Tobias Fox, I have a note for you from Harry Lime'.

It read:

MEET ME ON THE FERRIS WHEEL AT THE PRATER TOMORROW 8PM

Tobias was not surprised. It was the melodramatic gesture that suited Harry Lime.

'Is the Prater far from here Madam Glock?'

'Twenty minutes by taxi,' she replied.

On the following day the group stayed together. The hotel had a small dining room, and the host served wholesome fare. There were three requests for interviews by journalists, but Tobias fielded them with a simple press release.

At 7.30pm Tobias left the hotel. He walked up to Phila Moniker Street to the taxi rank outside the Sacher Hotel.

The Prater Amusement Park was dominated by the giant Ferris wheel that provided sweeping views of the city. It was a chilly night, with occasional drizzle and the crowd was sparse. Tobias sat at a coffee stall and took in the sights. He wished to ensure he was not being followed.

31

BERLIN

Chief Inspector Savvas Christou and Inspector Millie Geiger had been busy. Two days passed since Christou met the Cabinet. They compared notes.

'We can provide an interim report to our masters,' said Savvas Christou.

'They will not like what they read,' replied Millie Geiger.

'So be it,' he answered.

The detectives immediately after being briefed, 48 hours before, left a team of officers to conduct interviews and search the Chancelry. They drove to the Clinic. They found the private wardroom where Heinrich Beck was housed. There was an elderly couple fussing around a young man whose head was swaddled in bandages and who was crawling around the floor. He had a dummy in his mouth but occasionally he would spit it out and begin jabbering. It sounded like 'Mmmmm Bbbbb Ddddd', but it was meaningless. He caught sight of Millie Geiger and became excited. He called out 'MMmunmmy'.

This is a surprising turn of events', said Savvas Christou.

'Liar', Millie Geiger replied.

They introduced themselves to Beck's parents. Arnpo Beck was sober. This was unusual. He was drunk daily. Sobriety left him confused and angry. His wife, Lydie, was following her son, retrieving the dummy, as he crawled around the floor. She stood and shook hands with the officers.

'They have destroyed him. What are you going to do about Dr Merz. The man is a fiend.'

The detectives looked at one another. Savvas Christou nodded impassively to Lydie. Diplomacy was required. The parents of the fellow did not need to know their interest in his welfare was no more than marginal and on the periphery of their enquiries. They were searching for a document and a barber.

'Who were your son's friends in Berlin Mrs Beck? Did he keep in contact with you? Did he tell you of his life in Berlin?' Millie Geiger spoke in a gentle tone, but it was also clear she was a figure of authority. She required answers.

'He used to ring me every week,' said Lydie Beck, 'he is a good boy. He found it hard to make friends in Berlin. He was in the Hitler Youth when he was at home, but in Berlin he spent his time working in the Chancelry. He told me he had been given secret work by Minister Goebbels. He was required to spend evenings at a club known as The Lady Windermere. He did say he made some friends at the club'.

"Was your son a homosexual?' asked Millie.

Arnpo Beck became agitated and angry.

'What are you saying? My son is no schwul pussy. You look like a man. Perhaps you are a pillow princess.'

His wife quietened him down and the detectives quickly exited.

As they walked down the corridor Lydie Beck came out of the wardroom and ran after them. She grabbed Millie Geiger's arm.

'I believe my son was sexually confused. He talked of spending time with two friends he met at the Lady Windermere cabaret. He did not tell me their names, but he did say they were not German. He may have said English – but I am not sure. They were a man and a woman. The way he spoke I thought he may have been attracted to the man.'

She turned and hurried back to her husband and son.

The dectives drove to the Lady Windermere that evening. The barman was a wealth of information. Savvas showed him a photo of Heinrich Beck.

'Oh yes, I know the bugger, at least I think he is a bugger, if he is not a bugger he would not be here. He sat at the bar and stared at Harry Lime's party. Harry Lime has a permanent table at the far end of the room. You are both Bulle. You must have heard of Harry Lime.'

Millie Geiger looked at Savvas Christou. She had not heard of Harry Lime. Savvas simply nodded when the barman mentioned the name. She wondered if he was aware of Harry Lime. It was difficult for her to tell. She held her peace.

'Did he ever join Harry Lime's table', asked Savvas.

The barman thought this over. He began washing glasses. Savvas gave him a ten-mark note.

'I do not remember him ever talking to Harry Lime, but I saw him outside one night speaking to a couple of his crowd. One was a bugger, a real bugger, Larry Cromarty. The other was a girl singer Ronnie Tolar. They are Englanders or Americanos. Oh yes and I remember one night he was deep in conversation with that old sot Tobias Fox. He is a Scottish Whisky salesman.'

The barman ceased talking and went back to washing glasses. The well seemed to have dried up. The police officers turned to leave.

The barman stopped his work and spoke:

'We get a lot of soldiers in here. We even get people from the Chancelry. Why even Hitler's Barber used to come in with his mother. He is a strange young fellow. Somebody said he was touched. They were friends of Harry Lime.'

The detectives returned to the bar. If one well was dry another deeper well opened. Unfortunately, the barman knew little else.

'Harry Lime?' queried Millie as they drove back to police HQ.

'He is either a villain, a legend or a ghost', Savvas replied.

Their next stop was to the flat occupied by Ronnie Tolar and Larry Cromarty. Their apartment was empty. Two residents an elderly academic and his wife were questioned by the two officers.

'They have gone back to England,' the academic told them. He identified the photo of Beck. 'He was a new friend of Ronnie and Larry. Has he recovered?

'What do you mean? Was he sick?' asked Millie Geiger.

'So sick he was carted off by ambulance', said the old Professor.

The detectives produced a copy of the German identity card photo of Tom Wagner, but the Professor and his wife did not recognise him.

The next stop was the Wagner flat. Mutte was unimpressed by the visitors.

'How should I know where they have gone? For all I know the Nazis have locked them up?'

The two detectives brainstormed following a meeting with the Nazi Intelligence Service. They pieced together a profile of Tobias Fox. They joined the dots.

Savvas and Millie decided the party had probably left Berlin. 'Air, ship, road or rail' pondered Savvas. They set in motion teams of police to visit the wharf and airports. Another team sent off telegrams to police stations within 100km of Berlin informing them of the missing Barber asking that officers keep a look-out.

They made a trip to the Central Railway Station. A steward who had been on the train identified most of the group. He commented favourably on the singing of Veronika Veronika and the generosity of his gratuities from a man the officers assumed to be Tobias Fox.

A Cabinet meeting was organised. This was not difficult as the Ministers were all on tenterhooks since the Rommel letter went missing. There was hope, now dissipated, that Hitler may have mislaid it, but every cranny of his office was searched and searched again.

Savvas Christou brought Millie to the meeting. He introduced her to the Cabinet.

There were murmurings, 'a woman detective, have you no males,' 'a Greek and a woman no wonder there is crime.'

Savvas ignored the muttering.

'We now have a lot of detail about the events that led to the loss of the document, the missing barber and the harming of Heinrich Beck. There was a well formulated plot initiated by a man named Harry Lime to obtain the document. We believe he secured the services of a British Intelligence officer named Tobias Fox. We are not sure of the terms of engagement. Fox was able to obtain the assistance of Tom Wagner, the Barber. He acquiesced to avoid Dr Goebbels' plan to have Dr Merz conduct an operation on him to re-arrange his brain cells. The purpose of the operation was to demonstrate that brain power can be improved by rewiring the cells. The operation was eventually performed, in error, on a Chancelry employee named Heinrich Beck who was substituted for the Barber. It was disastrous. The man now has the mind of a baby. Tom Wagner's mother, the widow of a war hero, has left Berlin with her son. We have found notebooks belonging to Heinrich Beck. He was undertaking a clandestine investigation of the Wagner family. He had information they were partly Jewish. He was preparing to denounce them. Two English libertines, Ronnie Tolar and Larry Cromarty were enlisted by Tobias Fox to befriend and betray Heinrich Beck. The group left Berlin on a train. They are travelling as a musical troupe. The English girl Ronnie Tolar is pretending to be a singer named Veronika Veronika. Tobias Fox is playing the role of the impresario. The other members are acting in bit parts. We have no idea of the current whereabouts of Harry Lime.'

'And the Rommel Letter?' asked Martin Boorman.

'My appreciation of Harry Lime is that once he gets his hands on it, the letter will be sold to the highest bidder. He provides no favours to anybody but himself. However, the evidence suggests that either the Barber or Tobias Fox has the letter.'

'Do we know where they are in Vienna?' asked Boorman.

'They will not be hard to find,' Christou replied.

'Are you sure the English woman Ronnie Tolar is impersonating Veronika Veronika,' said Goring who today was clad in a sweeping ermine gown.

'I do not believe there is a singer named Veronika Veronika,' replied Christou blandly.

'Well, that is where you are wrong, very wrong,' Goring's face was a scarlet colour that matched the waistcoat under his ermine robe.

'There were SS officers on the train who recognised her from previous performances. There was even a former beau who knew her intimately.'

'So, he said,' interposed General Ribbentrop, who was well used to boasting officers.

Goring was concerned at the direction the discussion was headed. Hitler turned a blind eye to his delinquency, but he was aware Harry Lime possessed photos of him so lewd even the Fuehrer would have to act. So far Harry Lime's blackmailing had been limited to import licences and pardons, but this mess raised his jeopardy to a new level.

'We will look very silly if we raid a famous singer's retinue.' Goring said firmly.

Hitler rose,

'I have heard from Harry Lime. He contacted me by telephone. He claims my Barber stole the document and he is seeking to retrieve it. He makes the odd request that a concert be allowed to proceed in Vienna starring Veronika Veronika. He expects he will be able to hand over the letter after the concert. He wants 10,000US dollars for the letter. He also wants Marshall Goring to be my emissary in Vienna. I suggest our two police detectives accompany the Reich Marshall.'

Hitler left the meeting

The detectives drove back to HQ.

'This is bullshit,' said Millie Geiger.

'It is above our paygrade,' replied Savvas Christou, 'but at least we will get to enjoy a concert.

32

VIENNA

On the stroke of 8pm Tobias paid his fare and received his ticket to the Ferris wheel. He watched the giant conveyance stop and the sprinkle of passengers alight. Fresh ticket holders stepped into the wheel. Tobias waited until they all boarded. He entered the compartment. The sole occupant was Harry Lime. He stood, at the rear of the cabin, facing him.

'I have a plane organised to export the cargo. You will leave after the concert. You are likely to have some unwanted company. Goring has been delegated by Hitler to recover Rommel's report and arrest your group.'

Tobias was unworried. He had met many black-hearted men. Some could be trusted, others not. He took Harry Lime as a man of his word. He was clearly motivated by self-interest. He made this clear. It was the hand shakers and back slappers who were not to be trusted. 'If Harry Lime said he would extricate his party – he would.'

Both men watched the crowd below. There were the usual gaggle of Hitler youth jostling and upsetting people. Tobias saw one spit. The dollop of mucus landed at the feet of a young man dressed in Tyrolean hat and velvet coat. He was accompanied by a young woman in a billowing fancy skirt and the new heeled shoes. The young man smiled wanly and tipped his hat at the thug. Tobias growled but Harry Lime gave the hint of a smile:

'Force and anger often defeat gentility and grace.'

Tobias Fox knew that.

'It does not mean it is right.'

'No,' replied Harry, 'now do you have the Rommel letter.'

Tobias took the envelope out of the capacious pocket of his jacket. Harry Lime opened the envelope and carefully read the document.

'Excellent,' he said, 'now I need two copies. You will have to access a Gestetner. Here is the document back.'

Tobias had never used a Gestetner. He had seen photos and a news article describing the machine. It was an electric printing press that was said to be about to revolutionise printing. The report said it could be operated by a child.

'That was not part of the deal Lime. I do not know if there are any Gestetners in Vienna and if there are they would likely to be in Nazi Headquarters.'

Harry Lime was unperturbed.

'There is a Gestetner at the Central City Army HQ. Ronnie Tolar, or Veronika Veronika, as she has become, won the heart of a German officer on the train. She has his phone number. She should call him and arrange a dinner. Perhaps they can sup at the Opera House. She can plaintively wail that tickets are not selling well because of your incompetent failure to advertise the event widely. Leaflets should be distributed. Is there any way of printing them? The good Oberst will, no doubt, know of the Gestetner. He will surely direct a public officer to help her. My appreciation of Miss Tolar is that she is not simply fetching but is resourceful. I expect the task will be well within her capabilities. I need two copies. I will arrange that one of my men collect the documents from Miss Tolar. She will remember him. When they first met, he was an ambulance officer.'

Harry Lime walked towards the door of the Ferris wheel compartment and within seconds they reached the exit point. Tobias followed Harry Lime out of the wheel but within seconds Lime was swallowed up by the crowd.

Tobias Fox was not sure what to expect when he told Ronnie Tolar of her task, but she was excited and happy.

'A spy, I will be a spy like you and Harry Lime.'

'Harry Lime is no spy,' Tobias replied, 'he is a businessman. I suspect he is a new sort of businessman. One day the world will be full of Harry Limes.'

Ronnie phoned her Oberst and on the following evening they went to dinner. Tobias waited up for her to return.

'You are my old Father Bear, 'Ronnie chided, 'it was the first date. I told him he was fortunate that I did not bring a chaperone. We have arranged a second dinner on Sunday after the concert.'

'You will be gone,'

'He doesn't know that?','

'What about the Gestetner?'

'Oh that,' Ronnie flounced, 'I am printing the documents tomorrow. I told him more advertising leaflets were required. I blamed you. I said we needed the use of a Gestetner. We are concerned people will not know of our concert. I even sobbed.'

Oberst Werner Loev was looking forward to his next date with the beautiful singer Veronika Veronika. The Oberst saw himself as something of a lady's man. He enjoyed his reputation and sought to laugh it off when his fellow officers referred to him as Captain Casanova. He was pleased to help Veronika Veronika with her printing request. He had no knowledge of Gestetner machines other than they were sprouting in large Army offices wherever he travelled. Their use was in the hands of underlings, mainly women Army civil employees. He enlisted the aid of one of the secretarial staff and they stood at the door of the front office at HQ waiting for Veronika Veronika. She arrived in a car driven by one of Harry Lime's henchmen. It was the man who drove the ambulance in Berlin. He made a fuss of leaping from the automobile and opening the rear door for Ronnie. She alighted with the aid of his outstretched arm. When she saw her Oberst, she squealed in delight and ran to him. She hugged him briefly and planted a lipstick kiss on his cheek. The secretary watched with interest. She was a foolish young Viennese girl with her head in the clouds. Just looking at Veronika Veronika gave her goose bumps. 'Oh, if this could be me', she thought.

They passed through the typing pool into the back room where the Gestetner was housed. Werner left them, shooed away by the young typist.

'I will look after the lady,'

The Oberst went back to the garrison in his chauffeured car. He was looking forward to a second date with Veronika Veronika. 'Who knows what will occur?'

The Gestetner was turned on and Ronnie Tolar stood by watching, as if in awe, at the young secretary's dexterity. On the day before a hard-faced butch woman came to their hotel.

'I am an employee of Harry Lime. I am here to explain the workings of the Gestetner.'

Ronnie was interested to check if the reality matched the diagrams. She was relieved to find the buttons and levers were as she had been shown.

When the machine was turned on a sample leaflet was printed from the document she brought with her.

Ronnie, now Veronika Veronika, suddenly began wiping her forehead with her hanky.

'I feel faint. My rehearsals were very tiring. I am sorry but would you mind getting me a glass of water and perhaps a headache tablet,'

The girl was happy to be of assistance. Goodness knows she may even be given a ticket to the show. When she left, Ronnie Tolar took the concert leaflet out of the machine and inserted the Rommel paper in the slot. She printed two copies and stored the pages in her bodice. She re-inserted the concert leaflet and went back to wiping her brow. The girl returned with a young man.

'Our medical officer,' she said.

Ronnie drank from the glass of water given to her by the girl. She took in the doctor. He was looking at her with undisguised admiration. Ronnie Tolar became the essence of Veronika Veronika. She had not forgotten the art of coquetry. If she did not bat her eyelids, she practically did. The young secretary said later, 'she might as well have dropped her pants for the silly blighter.'

Soon enough Veronika Veronika was half-carried to the waiting car by the doctor and typist. A Staff Sergeant who was fresh from Berlin watched. He was a young man of libidinous tastes and a frequenter of The Lady Windermere in Berlin.

'She looks like the girl at the Club in Berlin who hangs around with Harry Lime, might be a relation'.

Veronika Veronika was bundled into the waiting car.

'I will take the lady to her hotel would you mind leaving the leaflets at the Box Office,' Harry Lime's driver said before he drove away.

'Have you got the papers?' he asked as soon as he turned the first corner.

'Of course,' Ronnie Tolar replied, putting the documents on the dash.

She was dropped at the hotel. Veronika Veronika nee Ronnie Tolar was looking forward to a stiff drink.

Harry Lime phoned Minister Goring.

'Reich Marshall', he said, 'I have Rommel's missing document. It is most illuminating. I look forward to the war. My sales thrive when legal supplies are low. I also have a bonus for you. You may remember the young boy you rodigered at the Countess Von Zerremer's soiree. I have obtained a photo of the performance. You really need to lose weight Herman, the sight of you is quite disgusting. Your schwarz is a tiny little fellow even when in full flower. I will throw in the film once the money is deposited in my Swiss Account. I told Hitler not to use Reich Marks. They are play-money. Pay in US dollars. You will receive the document on the night of the concert in Vienna. It will do you good to absorb some culture. You will be informed at the concert how to obtain the Rommel report and your photos. I should not have to tell you, but if you disrupt the concert Berlin will be flooded with your disgusting pictorials'.

Harry Lime hung up. He did not wait for an answer.

33

BERLIN - VIENNA

Marshall Goring travelled to Vienna in the official
express luxury train built for the Fuehrer and
the other members of the Cabinet. Police Inspectors
Savvas Christou and Millie Geiger were onboard. The
Marshall handpicked fifty of his officers to accompany
him. They arrived the day before the concert and the
Concert Hall was extensively and fruitlessly searched.

Tobias Fox watched from a distance. He was
unworried by the activity. Veronika Veronika
rehearsed her songs at the hotel accompanied by her
pianist Tom Wagner.

A support act was engaged. The Viennese counter
tenor choir was to perform. Their performances in
Berlin were lauded both by music critics and the
doctors who practised Eugenics. There were some
murmurings, 'if you want to hear a boys' choir use real
boys not disfigured men and call them castratos for
that is what they are.'

The night of the concert arrived.

The vocal group had a following in their
hometown. Apart from friends and relatives they were
supported by the homosexual community that had

become more visible since Hitler's rise to power. It is doubtful if the Veronika Veronika handouts sold many tickets but there were a few Viennese who attended every concert. The Luftwaffe officers, all in civilian garb, were seated on the aisles and though the theatre was not sold out there was a respectable crowd.

Goring was only seated momentarily when one of his men approached.

'I was told to give this to you,' the man said. It was a crumpled piece of paper. It read:

COME STRAIGHT TO THE PRATER –
THE MOUSE WILL GIVE YOU FURTHER
DIRECTIONS.

Goring rose. 'Get me my driver and those Berlin detectives immediately.'

Within a minute the staff car was on its way to the amusement park. On arrival they entered and took in the surrounds. It was early evening so there was still only a small crowd of pleasure seekers. There were carnival rides, fairy floss stalls and freak shows. The group stood at the entrance while Goring considered his next move. Finally, a human sized brown mouse walked up. The mouse, or more accurately, the person in the mouse suit spoke to Goring.

'Ride on the Ferris wheel. The documents will be waiting for you.'

Goring summonsed the two detectives.

'Come with me.'

They arrived at the giant wheel, then claimed to be the largest in Europe. It was slowly turning. Finally, it came to a halt and the crowd disbursed into the park. Goring did not notice the man in the black homburg hat in the middle of the departing crowd. There were few customers for the next ride. The attendant summonsed Goring.

'Your carriage Excellency.'

Goring gestured to Christou and Geiger.

'Go, there will be two envelopes in the cabin.'

The Reich Marshall was now afraid of heights. He was an ace pilot in World War 1, but suddenly he found himself shaking and sweating at the mere thought of flying. He only travelled by plane, these days, when stoked on pills or sozzled on alcohol. This was not difficult as he was usually wrecked in one way or the other. Tonight, he knew he must be sober. The future of the Third Reich and more importantly his own reputation hung in the balance.

The detectives boarded the wheel, and it commenced its turn. There were two envelopes on the seat. One had written on the front the words 'Rommel's Report'. The other was blank. Christou opened the plain envelope. He handed it to Inspector Millie Geiger. She looked at the contents and handed it back to Christou.

'These photos are disgusting. I heard the Reich Minister was a lecher but gorgonzola and apple sauce, the man is a monster.'

Christou put the photos back in the envelope and placed it in his pocket.

'What are you doing?' Millie asked.

'Insurance,' replied Christou.

When the wheel reached the ground, they alighted, and Christou gave the Rommel's Report to Goring.

'Was there only one envelope?' he asked.

'Yes,' the detectives replied, in unison.

At the Concert Hall the crowd was rapturous. Veronika Veronika was in the wings listening to the applause that greeted her first encore when Tobias Fox walked over.

'Time to leave,' he said.

Veronika Veronika was momentarily reluctant until Larry Cromarty said, 'Ronnie Tolar are you coming or not.'

The party ran into the bowels of the auditorium. There was a grate open in the stone floor. They clambered down the single stairs into the sewage tunnel system of Vienna. Tobias was last to leave shutting the grate as he clambered down the stairs. The group made their way gingerly along the side path of the rushing sewer. Larry Cromarty led the way, followed by Sarah and Tom Wagner, Ronnie Tolar and Tobias Fox.

They heard clanking machinery and rushing water. They reached the sewage ponding system. The sewage was reticulated and treated before being disgorged into the river system. Tobias moved to the front.

'Follow me.' He said as he led the group through a gap in the wall into a narrow tunnel where treated water was apparently expelled. They saw moonlight. A man was waiting with a rowboat.

'Clothes off,' he said, 'I am not having my plane stinking from shit.'

The group rowed to a Catalina flying boat. They boarded and the plane set off down the Danube Canal, rose into the air and turned to head West.

On his rowboat, in the shadows of a pier, an old fisherman, angling for carp, watched the departure. He left the jetty and went to the phone box in the street adjacent to the Canal. He rang the police.

'I just saw some naked people rowing in the Canal,' he told the Police officer, 'they got into a boat plane and took off.'

'Did you see the flying pig as well,' answered the incredulous police officer.

34

CHEQUERS – SCOTLAND

It was early afternoon when Lancet arrived at Chequers. Churchill was resting on his ottoman clad in a corduroy dressing gown.

'Well done, Lancet. I trust everybody is safe and sound,'

'Thank you, Winston, do you have the report?'

'It was worth every penny Lancet; I am garnering support as we speak.'

Lancet resisted the temptation to comment on the old Statesman's garb.

'That fellow Fox did a sterling job. Shall I recommend a K.'

'I think not, Winston, he craves anonymity.'

'Is the German General still in place? You seem to have protected his cover.' There was a twinkle in Winston's eyes.

'What General,' replied Oliver Lancet.

Tobias Fox was back in Scotland. He sat on a plank chair on the veranda of his cottage. The wood paling outer walls were mottled and bruised by the years of rain, sleet and hail that tested their mettle. As Tobias leant back in his chair the floor groaned in sympathy. He sucked on his briar pipe and breathed out a gust of aromatic tobacco.

He knew Sarah would soon pop out of the front door with his morning coffee. When the door opened, he would hear Ronnie and young Tom practising in the back room for their forthcoming concert tour. 'Veronika Veronika, the toast of Europe accompanied by the gifted young pianist Tom Wagner.' Perhaps he would hear their manager Larry Cromarty shout that he had a new booking. His literary pursuits were now forgotten as he reinvents as a theatrical agent. Sure, enough he heard the creaking sounds of steps on the floorboards and Sarah Wagner appeared. The bracing Scottish air agreed with her.

Tobias took another puff and leant back to take in the view. The shack was in the lee of the hills that stretched out like a row of crazy steps with their black crags and green dales. There were herds of woolly sheep dotting the lower steppes and as the hills rose there was the occasional white cap where snow rested. As he gazed at the view, he never tired of watching, his eyes were drawn to the road at the end of the property driveway. It was a narrow shale snake of a blacktop. It wound its way down the valley to the Speyside waterfront where the whisky was distilled, bottled and sent on its merry way to every corner of the globe. A vehicle could be seen huffing and puffing its way up the hill. Tobias recognised the conveyance. It was the taxi operated by Finlay Foote. Speyside's only taxi. He wondered if it was coming for him. Was Oliver Lancet tired of waiting for a de-briefing? Finlay may be heading further up the hill.

The widow McGlashan in the farm above may have some business in Aberdeen or Jock the shearer might be coming to comb the wool.

Tobias was wrong. The taxi turned into the drive and unhappily chugged up the hill to rest outside the veranda not ten feet from where Tobias was seated. The door opened and a young woman alighted.

'Do you remember me. I am Poppy Schafer', she said, 'I have come to see Tom Wagner. I heard he is here.'

'I was expecting you', Tobias said,

Poppy was carrying a small cardboard suitcase. Tom took the case and escorted her into the house. Sarah hugged her and led her into the backroom. Tom Wagner was sitting at his piano. He was excited.

'Where have you been? How did you find me? How did you come here?'

Sarah calmed him.

'All in good time, give the girl a chance to become acclimatised'.

Tobias Fox put on his windcheater and tartan cap with the built in earmuffs. He clambered onto his BSA motor bike and set off for Speyside. It was time to go back to work. His brothers had been sympathetic when he returned from Vienna.

'Take your time, we have plenty of stock of single malt, we can also sell our blends'.

They must have been intrigued by his new family.

'Was the woman his lover, surely not Tobias, he was the epitome, the very boggle of a bachelor'.

'And the young bonnie lad and lassie who were they? The Sassenach sissy boy was the lassie's manager, they knew that much. Then there were the occasional

visitors from London in suits and cashmere overcoats.'
The Speyside pubs were beset by rumours.

While Tobias was heading down the hill, Poppy
was giving Tom the abridged version of her path
to Scotland. She was always an independent soul.
She had to be.

After her hurried departure from the Chancelry
she realised she had burnt her bridges. Anyway, Tom
was gone. She took a familiar route and made her way
back to Alsace-Lorraine. The border was porous and
as she spoke French like a native, as all the residents
of the border region did, she got work as a maid in
a small town. She saved her money and travelled to
Paris. By now the city was in peril and the Parisians
knew it. Without quite knowing why she found a
berth on a cruise ship whose first stop was London.
Poppy left the ship in London to take in the sights.
She spoke and read a little English. She read an article
in a giveaway paper that reported Veronika Veronika,
formerly Ronnie Tolar, recently performed at a club
in Soho accompanied by her pianist, Tom Wagner.
Ronnie Tolar, the girl from the Lady Windermere; She
was a singer. The coincidence was too great. She did
not know Tom was a musician, but, for some reason,
it did not surprise her. She left the ship to look for
Tom. She remembered the name Tobias Fox. He was
easy enough to track down and soon enough she was
on her way to Speyside,

Tobias turned the corner to the row of dockside
sheds and drove into the distillery. His brothers must
have heard his approach, and they were waiting for him.

'Harry Lime is inside,' said Eamon, the eldest.

Harry Lime was dressed in his usual black suit and long cashmere coat. He carried his Homburg hat.

'What are you doing here?' asked Tobias.

'I have come to thank you. The Rommel papers have been a fine investment. I sold the original back to the Nazis and the copies to your side. I sold one to Stanley Baldwin and this caused him to resign. He was sure before then Hitler was a man of his word, and he realised he was duped. I sold the second copy to Churchill, and this helped to persuade him to give up painting streams and save the country. I have never liked that fellow Oliver Lancet, so I let slip how you were misused by the man. He will be put out to pasture when Churchill is ready. As far as you are concerned, you must diversify. A world war is coming, and the soldiers will need antiseptic fluid for their wounds. The blending is quite complex, and you are well placed to carry out the contract. I have placed a large order with your brothers'.

'But if war breaks out, we cannot send goods to Austria or Germany'.

'I am based in Valparaiso. It will be neutral. I intend to supply both sides.'

Harry Lime departed in his usual manner – a black clad, backseat passenger in a black limousine.t. Tobias recognised the driver and passenger from an ambulance ride in Berlin not long ago.

A wharf rat who occasionally did some labouring for the distillery put his head in the doorway and almost screamed at the three brothers.

'Hitler has invaded Poland. The war has begun.'

ABOUT THE AUTHOR

The author has practised as a barrister, KC, Judge and Law Professor over a career spanning 50 years. He is also a musician and songwriter. He is the Jazzer in the Rocker & Jazzer band that has recorded several albums and co-written numerous songs that have been covered in the USA and Europe. He has written two published textbooks and a memoir, REFLECTIONS OF TINY VICTORIES. His fiction JERRY O, MONKEY MAN, BARBED WIRE, THE PONIARD BLADE and SNIPPETS OF OTHER LIVES are available in print. His short stories have been published in National periodicals.